EXHUMED

EXHUMED

13 TALES TOO TERRIFYING TO STAY DEAD

A Gravelight Press Postmortem Offering

Exhumed: 13 Tales Too Terrifying to Stay Dead

Designed and edited by David Yurkovich.

Excepting the introduction, the works within this collection were originally published in the Devil's Party Press anthologies *Halloween Party 2017*, *Aurora*, and *Halloween Party 2019*.

Special thanks to Jeffrey D. Keeten for providing a killer introduction, and to the authors who allowed their work to live again by way of this collection.

gravelightpress.com

ISBN: 978-1-7340918-1-6

CONTENTS

"I think perhaps all of us go a little crazy at times."

Robert Bloch, *Psycho*

EXHUMED

INTRODUCTION

Jeffrey D. Keeten

WHAT WE LIKE ABOUT HORROR is the way fear lights up our brains like a pinball machine on tilt and forces us to feel more alive. It is like driving fast along a dark road in a 1955 Ford Thunderbird with the top down and the headlights off. You've got Bill Haley & His Comets playing on the radio. A pretty girl with a cherry-tipped cigarette dangling from her lips is hanging her long legs out the passenger-side window. Then you go into a skid, gravel sprays, and with heart racing you see something blacker than the night coming straight at you.

We are all lead characters in the novels of our lives, and reading horror adds zesty, vicarious moments of apprehension to our plots. Robert Louis Stevenson deploys a magnificent sense of dread by describing how Mr. Hyde comes alive in Dr. Jekyll: "That insurgent horror was knit to him closer than a wife, closer than an eye; lay caged in his flesh, where he heard it mutter and felt it struggle to be born." Reading horror is like that for me, awakening something raw and primeval buried deep within.

The terror that reading tales of horror inspires does not stay locked in our minds, carefully controlled like a caged beast, but escapes into the shadowy nooks of our dwellings, to lodge in the creak on the stairs and unsettle us with the tap tap tap on the window glass. The disturbing images writers put in our heads bleed into our real universe. So readers caught in the web of another's imagination must be prepared to have their senses expand and possibly even glimpse out of the corner of their eyes the manifestation of the fears that a talented writer has conjured for them. These are shared fears; the writer is taking her worst anxieties and infecting her readers with fresh nightmares.

We have 13 tales in this anthology, an unnerving baker's dozen. These stories have all been published in other anthologies, which means they survived the cut against hundreds of other contenders, and then they withstood yet another rigorous selection process when Gravelight Press chose the very best of them. Congratulations to all the writers. As happy as these 13 writers are, you, as a reader, should be even happier. This stringent process has ensured that you will be chilled, thrilled, and thoroughly entertained.

What I especially appreciate about this collection is that Gravelight Press, like its parent company Devil's Party Press, only accepts stories from writers who are likely to be suffering from Dickensesque gout, Poe's anxiety, and achromotrichia. In other words, the writers are all over 40. They have endured the trials and tribulations of their youth and now, with a plethora of real life experiences lining the bookshelves of their minds (think Green Apple Books in San Francisco or The Strand in New York), they are able to leaf through their memories to add nuances to their stories that only those with wise eyes can share.

So what are these stories about?

There are monsters—beautiful ones, fanged ones, hairy ones, and even a *Frankensteined* Santa Claus that will soon become a staple in the Keeten household over the holidays. There are zombies, ghostly creatures, and an eggplant *shiver* cassoulet. There is the creature feature town of Stumpville, and if I ever have to visit there, I'll be sure to keep Dean and Sam Winchester on speed dial. There is a sandcastle imbued with supernatural power. There is a Halloween seamstress who creates shivers with her skills. There are haunting pieces of writing that leave residual trails of horror in my brain, like, "Your skeleton becomes a perilous snag." Or how about a little taste of Franz Kafka with "exoskeletons clicked like castanets"? There is a hoarsely whispered mantra that will make your ears tingle: "Mothers can be tricky. Daughters can be slippery."

This book also provides helpful hints. For instance, should I ever find myself a member of the walking dead and embarrassed by the stench escaping my rotting corpse, I will be sure to put "pine tree fresheners in the pockets of my blazer to hide my rotten egg smell." Ha! Brilliant! There is also plenty of shared wisdom about what *not* to do, and isn't that another reason we read tales of horror or watch the latest installment of *Friday the 13th*? We are seeking enlightenment as well as entertainment. We like to ask ourselves, *What would I do? I sure as heck wouldn't open that door leading to the creepy basement or hide out in the barn with all the pointy things hanging from the rafters.* We know bad things happen in those circumstances because horror has provided us with those insights.

I think it is important to set the mood properly to fully enjoy the stories you are about to read. I read them late at night, long after everyone else had gone to bed, and I could hear every creak and moan from the house. The wind just happened to be blowing, jangling loose things and rattling the eves. I lit candles to add those dancing shadows to the room. I poured two fingers of 10-year-old Scotch. A reader must be properly fortified. I sat in the safe pool of my reading light and let these stories play like flickering movies in my head.

I hope you all enjoy being unsettled by these tales as much as I did. May your dreams be spiked by joyous moments of terror.

Dodge City, Kansas
August 2020

...AND ALL THE TRIMMINGS

J.C. Raye

PROFESSOR NORMAN TACK sat very still inside the oversized tow sack as the little creatures bore him away across the frosty, December evening sky, surely bound for what would be a grave, if not unpleasant, incomprehensible fate. While other abductees might have shouted and flailed or set about ingeniously transforming a stainless-steel pen into an improvised weapon in preparation for a daring Hollywoodesque escape, such was not the case with Norman. It simply was not in Norman's makeup to do so. He was a thinker. A theorist. Not so much a coward. The details were always such a distraction for the man, always inhibiting any decisive or compelling action on his part. Instead of worrying *where* they might be taking him, or *what* actually took him, at this moment, the professor was genuinely trying to place the pungent odor of the scratchy fabric surrounding him. An endless ride of jolts and jerks in complete and terrifying blackness, the assurance of yet another herniated disc in the near future, while Norman inhaled big whiffs of air, trying to decide between paint varnish or graham crackers.

Professor Tack was lovingly referred to by both students and colleagues alike as *Tic-Tack*. He'd inherited the nickname either because of an unmistakable, square, pale head, or the irritating but reliable chatter of boxed breath mints that emanated from the pocket of his tan corduroy jacket on any given day. Presently he was not even leaning toward the casting of blame, as most would in this scenario. Certainly, a dramatic, rather supernatural—and very public—kidnapping on a medium-sized college campus like Carroll University might not have occurred if the school grounds had been equipped with adequate lighting, or if a single security officer had been present on the long path back to the west faculty lot. And yes, there were others on the walkway who might have served as more enchanting victims. Several attractive yet unattached coeds had been milling about, cluelessly texting on their cells, each no doubt capable of emitting a blood-curdling scream. There had also been older, tenured, more cadaverous colleagues tottering out to their strategically parked Audis in the furthest regions of the lot. These, the creatures might have swept away with ease and, conceivably, procured a booty of greenbacks and a Rolex in the process. Norman, therefore, concluded that the little *jabbas* must have wanted *him*, specifically, as they scooped him up and plunked him into their sack. He didn't fuss then, and he wasn't fussing now. Unwisely perhaps, he was more curious than anything else.

Jabbas. Norman's first impression. Firing into his grey matter the instant they effortlessly floated down from the foliage in wooly three-piece suits, to surround him on the gravel. Indeed, they reminded him of the repulsive alien-gangster from the *Star Wars* mythos. Noggins shaped like slowly melting chocolate kisses, and wide slit-eyes, gleaming golden, which erupted from thick folds of moist amphibian skin. In all honestly, these were far less intimidating than the movie character, as not a one of the creatures rose over two and a half feet tall. There was also that added, innocuous, sugar-plum coloring which made them almost doll-like. Dolls with the strength of sumo wrestlers who had mastered the power of flight.

———

Hands clasped behind his back, bedecked in a velvet, burgundy dressing gown with a quilted emerald green silk collar, Norman turned circles on the tufted rug in front of a crackling fire in the great reading room. As he travelled, he stared down and scowled at twin idiotic snowman faces crocheted into the slipper socks the jabbas had bestowed upon him. Seven pairs in all. These, the least emasculating. Norman's patience waned. It was a new and altogether disturbing emotion for the 60-year-old humanities lit professor.

It seemed to Norman that the Christmas elves (he knew this now) had kept him captive a little more than two weeks. *Certainly, the remaining days until the holiday must be few*, Norman thought. Yet to his great dismay, this unspecific supposition was the very limit of how certain he could be about the passage of time during his captivity. Norman was losing track of the days. Not at all surprising and completely forgivable, when one's surroundings no longer included the customary, recognizable patterns and mechanisms that parceled out normal human existence. The rooms he was allowed to see were bereft of clocks and calendars. From what Norman could fathom, his pint-sized captors, (beyond numbering in the hundreds) also bore no timepieces, whether wrapped around chubby eggplant wrists or dangling from a fob chained to a cherry-red waistcoat. And, though all the rooms featured towering windows, as befitting a Gothic Santa Clausian estate, none were transparent. Norman noted that the windows were not glass but a type of iron-hard colored ice, which never indicated any change of light outside, whether dawn or dusk. Each window a unique stained glass depiction that included colorful background details—decorations, lights, and all the trimmings. Strategic shards weaving the glory of Santa. Flying the sled over a beaming yellow moon. Feeding reindeer. Descending from a chimney. Visiting joyful children in faraway lands. The renderings reminded Norman of the stained glass Stations of the Cross he'd seen portrayed in churches.

These creatures, Norman concluded, seemed to have power over ice, snow, and water. He did not really notice it when they appropriated him against his will. Too much to take in then. He had assumed they were floating or flying. At closer inspection later, he observed their power of flight to be manufactured by a steady spool of churning ice crystals beneath their feet. Infinitesimal. Soundless. Serving any whim, at any speed, and in any direction. The unbreakable windows, many of the door locks, and even the fireplace were mystifying and fantastic examples of this strange technology. The fire looked and acted like a fire. It emanated heat and dispensed the traditional blend of colors, pops and sizzles. Yet, it was made entirely of ice and, therefore, required neither a refreshment of logs nor supervision. Norman assumed that Santa and the elves had avoided detection by utilizing this same unnerving skill. *Perhaps this entire estate is safely tucked inside an ice mirage of some kind*, he thought.

Norman was allowed unlimited access to this space, a great reading room, via a connecting door to his bedroom. This room, undoubtedly the man cave of Old Saint Nick. It was by the far the grandest part of the compound. The enormous rectangular room was filled floor to ceiling with bookshelves containing several thousand hardcovers that were inserted into an ocean of shining Italian walnut linenfold panels. In the center of each panel, an emblem of holly had been etched. A brightly painted fresco of fir branches adorned the 15-foot-high ceiling. Norman felt that it provided the room with a kind of *protected* feeling, and a sense of comfort and warmth, despite the fearsome tempests beyond the walls which howled constantly. At least Norman *assumed* it was a storm outside, and not an insistent chorus of hungry wolves requesting a raw elf dinner, but he had no way of knowing.

Eight interior columns flanked the longer walls. Exquisite carvings of poinsettia garlands were twisted around each like the stripe on a candy cane. The leather chairs were wide and comfortably broken in. Drapes and their tiebacks, however, were noticeably absent, perhaps to prevent detainees from inflicting self-harm.

The focal point of the space was the massive fireplace at one end of the vast chamber. Reliefs of toys were hand-carved into the yellow marble. Norman counted four dozen in all. Each figure was so punctiliously sculpted into the stone, that from afar, it seemed the toys might snap to life at any moment and leap down from their station to freedom. The mantle reached well above 12 feet, above which hung a strange coat of arms that appeared to have been constructed of a mixed media rather than pure metal. A trickle of dried skins hung from the coat, and from this Norman could only assume that Santa, in his spare time, was a small game hunter. *Everyone's got their vices*, he mused.

Reading was a most powerful distraction from Norman's piteous circumstance. Norman attributed his constant physical pain and the increasing ache in his scalp to be the result of an allergic reaction or blossoming infection caused by either the plucking of all his native sandy brown hair or the expedited 10,000 hair grafts of white llama hair which followed, expedited over his first four agonizing days in captivity. The elves, it seems, were unaware of ibuprofen. They did, however, recognize suffering, and were quick to provide their custom icepacks following any of Norman's many surgeries.

The library books were Norman's means to self-heal. He soon discovered that the library collection was more than just eclectic, it was astonishing. Among the many delightful items on its ledges were a 15th century *Book of Lismore*, a *Gutenberg Bible*, and the *Codex Leicester* by Leonardo Da Vinci. Norman almost mistook Leonardo's rose-colored tome for a placemat while looking to set down his daily mug of mulled cider. A colleague at Carroll had shared with him years ago that only one such copy existed, the original, penned single-handedly by the mathematician himself, and acquired by Bill Gates in the 1990s. Norman had no idea whether any of these books were copies or originals, obtained legally or criminally. For all he knew, Santa was a closet biblioklept.

In the early days of this compulsory call, farthest from the fireplace, and deep in shadows at the back of the great library, Norman found a section of books that seemed a mismatch, a subdivision of sorts, almost at odds with the room itself. These shelves were a disorganized mess, and clearly a signpost of steady activity outside of his peaceful visiting hours. Here, books were tipped over onto their sides or half pulled away from their ledges. Large piles stacked haphazardly crowded the floor, surrounded by others splayed open with pages bent or torn, looking as if they had been carelessly lobbed from several feet away.

The professor picked up one of these and scanned its cover. Upon inspection, Norman noticed that these were not bound books, but leather journals with buckle closures, though many of the straps were missing as a result of their apparent abuse. The brown leather was hard and thick, perhaps buffalo rather than goat or cowhide. The front of the journal contained a rendering of a toy soldier that had been meticulously embossed into the grain. Inside the journal, Norman found step-by-step instructions describing how to make the toy. No words or text. No table of contents. Only diagrams and drawings. The last few pages featured color palettes and strokes specific to the painting of eyes, shoes, and uniform. Norman tucked the journal neatly back onto a shelf and selected one that teetered on a ledge.

Norman looked over his shoulder to confirm that he was still alone, uncertain how his little *friends* might respond to an outsider spying on trade secrets. Then again, Norman reasoned, creatures who trimmed their toenails with their teeth were not likely beleaguered by the concept of intellectual property being stolen out from under them. This second journal was much chunkier. Spinning tops in tin and wood, and a vast array of painted design samples. Everything from cowboys to ballerinas to astronauts to dinosaurs. Other journals he found, on higher shelves and coated in dust, were those of what Norman assumed to be toy concepts that had lost their popularity, such as wind-up racecars or wooden horses with wheeled feet.

Norman concluded that these journals had been prepared by Santa. He now made a rather exhilarating connection. Norman recalled that several days ago, face deep in *Arabian Nights*, he heard a breathy exhalation behind him. He'd looked up to see an elf, rather lanky, but with a slightly oversized cranium, just inside the paneled door, observing him quite strangely. Norman had smiled at the creature, nodded and held his book aloft as if to express his enjoyment of it. The elf regarded him for a moment more, then placed his hands on his hips, shook his head, and left the room. *That was it.* The jabba did not seem to understand the concept of reading. Perhaps Claus quietly suppressed this skill, fearing it would result in reduced productivity.

—

Two days after they removed his nose and replaced it with that of a crimson-faced *uakari* monkey, the combination of itch and throb in Norman's snout could not be satiated by another afternoon of Melville, Austin, Tolstoy. Norman headed over to the north wing with a hankering for Yorkshire pudding, and maybe a bit of treacle sponge cake. If there were any benefits at all to being slowly torn asunder, body part by body part, and *Frankensteined* into a Santa Claus (which he now assumed was happening) it was the food. A feast was ongoing at any time of day. Not a meal. A *feast*. The likes of which King Henry Tudor might have drooled over. Trifle, custards, cookies, and cakes. Duchess potatoes soaked in butter. Roasted brussels sprouts. Cranberry and chestnut salad. Glazed ham and beef Wellington. Roast duckling. Stuffed capons.

Apparently, the elves worked in rotating shifts to ensure that Santa's dining hall was always set for a scrumptious repast. The creatures also seemed to eat in shifts as well. Day and night, the hall was jammed with their smelly purple selves, elbow to elbow, deafeningly blabbering away in their slushy, phlegmy, undecipherable mother tongue. Norman usually prepared a tray to take back to his bedroom, after spending a good deal of time searching for unmolested portions on the large serving platters, since the creatures were seemingly unaware of silverware or the decorum of chewing with lips zipped. The professor could have eaten 24 hours a day if he so fancied. Portion control supervision did not exist. No surprise there. Unless they were planning to use a tire inflator on his belly in the last hours before Christmas.

As he passed through the connecting hallway lined with thick timber beams and reindeer portraits, two of the jabbas burst out of the toy shop which was immediately to his right. One had a chisel handle protruding from his eye socket. His eye gushed purple elf juice all over the damn place. He chased the other with large red hand saw. Norman literally dove out of their way. Losing his balance, he painfully thumped his funnybone on the corner of Donner's likeness. His presence was unnoticed by the elves. The elf being chased shrieked in fear, and the other, unbelievably, still functioning with the business end of a metal chisel driven deeply into his skull, growled like a deranged hound. They soon disappeared down the hall.

But now, the toy shop, which Norman had never been allowed to see, was open. Consumed with their Two Stooges cabaret, neither elf had bothered to closed and lock the door. It was far too tempting.

—

A deep disappointment to be sure. Even though his rather lofty expectations of Santa's famous toy shop might very well have been pieced together from childhood memories of Rankin/Bass stop-motion animation. This was a mess. This was *wrong*. Overturned tables. Tools scattered along the floor. Spilled paint cans. Norman treaded carefully to avoid tripping. Near one of the many spills, little purple hands had finger painted a reindeer with three heads and a long penis with holly berries growing on it.

There were no complete toys to be found at all, only parts in progress, though some of the instructional journals from the library lay about as well. The finger painter seemed to have been working on these, too, penis theme persisting. Someone had painted a crooked checkerboard directly onto a table and used a hoard of doll's eyes as the pieces. Several shelves were cramped with rag dolls, piled and pushed onto each other in twos and threes. The dolls were missing arms, legs, and dresses and had been placed in disturbing positions. One had been crucified with pencils, a painted tear beneath one of her eyes. At the far end of the room, nails had been carefully driven into the wall in the shape of an elf's face that resembled Norman's lanky, cranium-endowed friend. It appeared as the nail outline was used for a game of rasp file darts. Someone had even thrown an axe.

Norman slipped on a paint can lid and lost his balance. Mid-flight, he caught the vision of a chisel hanging off a bench seat, fast approaching his face. His decision to attempt an army roll came late and failed for several reasons, not the least of which was the fact that Norman knew precious little about actually performing the maneuver. He fell hard and his shoulder landed directly inside an open box of tacks. A few of them stuck. His first thought was not registering new pain, but the fear he had somehow damaged his nose. He lifted his hand to check. All good. He then started to remove the little silver thumbtacks embedded in his flesh, using pliers to extract the stubborn ones. There was a bit of bleeding, and Norman spotted an overturned journal just under the table near him. Though not ideal, the loose pages would, Norman determined, be useful in blotting the blood.

———

It was not a mislaid instructional journal from the library at all. And it was *clearly* not authored by Santa. Jabba hand. Norman was quite sure it was never meant for his eyes. The first three-quarter cluster of pages was meticulously rendered; vivid colors, exquisite lines. This illuminated manuscript might have rivaled any medieval monk's sketchbook, stretching back in the elves' history to the time when Santa first brought them here. The renderings upon the weathered pages depicted hundreds of elves, chained together and attached to the tail of a very large beast, against a landscape that matched their coloring. If the professor had to liken the monster-jailor portrayed to any earthly animal, he might settle on the capybara, a South American desert rodent, but one that was over 80 feet long and weighed 300,000 pounds. Clearly under duress, the elves were churning up the ice under their feet to keep the beast cool. Drawings depicted other beasts scuttling about too. Skinnier ones, toothier ones, eating smaller jabbas, possibly elf children.

Turning the pages, Norman learned how Santa, under cover of night and in small groups, had chauffeured the elves away through the stars to bring them to his snowy sanctuary. The years that followed looked very happy, with elves being clothed, learning to cook, and blissfully crafting beautiful teddy bears and model trains while always, *always*, maintaining a blind deference to, and passionate admiration for, the man who had rescued them from space rodents. It was here, Norman noticed, that the pages had become dislodged. The leaves were handled. Crumpled. Stuffed in. The art chaotic, shoddy, with a touch of rage.

Apparently, Santa had gone through a change. Alzheimer's? Mental illness? Norman could not be sure. Illustrations showed the man wandering off naked into the hills and often breaking toys in anger. Pages and pages of elves being slapped, kicked, and pummeled. As the violence increased, so did the weapons of choice; whips, belts, mallets. A bloody scene laid out like a pornographic centerfold recounted the night Santa murdered all of the reindeer with an augur.

Norman did not really need to see the final pages, a helly and wholly predictable, *'Twas the Night*, surefire sequel, in which hundreds of jabbas finally maxed out on a life of pain, on *two* planets, took action. But like any worthwhile literature professor, he felt compelled to read the story to its end.

Norman dropped the journal and raced back to the library, his craving for Yorkshire pudding or other nourishment utterly forgotten.

—

Norman pushed the chair closer to the fireplace. He felt the heat intensify on his knees as he stood atop the chair. Not that it mattered. He needed a closer look.

Yes, they had done it. What he had mistaken for a rabbit or martin carcass slung over the coat of arms were, in fact, slices of dried human skin and century-old tangles of white curly hair. They had killed him. Killed him long ago. And had evidently enjoyed the killing. Had taken their time with each ritualistic slice of the vicious tyrant. Had revelled in the newfound freedom and the end to their endless nightmare.

Norman's mind worked quickly to assemble a puzzle that was forming in his mind but still lacking various pieces. After a time, he deduced, one of the elves, possibly the one with the large cranium, must have realized that the world might *miss* Santa or look for him. Maybe the elves thought everyone on Earth behaved like Santa and they'd be horribly punished. Maybe they feared the world would send another oppressor to take his place. In any case, Norman concluded that this was why they needed him. And others. Probably others too. *Each year.* They needed a Santa.

For the first time in weeks, Norman felt real fear. He also felt terribly decisive. Norman hopped down off the chair, resolving, for the first time in his life, to take a compelling action. *Of course,* Norman thought, *taking a compelling action is easier said than done when 12 purple chocolate kiss creatures topple you to the ground.* Because that's exactly what they did.

———

When they finally seated him in the wooden sleigh, Norman lacked even an ounce of resistance. Not that it mattered since he was outnumbered at least 50 to one. Norman knew without any doubt that his hour of reckoning was approaching. It seemed as if every resident had put down their figgy pudding pops and red-handled saws to see him off. Many helped load the countless toy sacks onto the sleigh. As the tears streamed down Norman's face–absorbed into the thick white llama beard only recently sewn into the fleshy part of his lower cheeks–he moaned horribly and pleaded for release. Of course, many of his words now were mostly unintelligible due to a current lack of dental fricatives. The elves then shoved a translucent rubber mouthpiece, slathered with a gelatinous and sticky goo, into his yowling mouth. A wide hole in the rubber enabled breathing between his gums.

Now Norman understood last night's dental visit, which had resulted in the removal of his teeth, one by excruciating one. His choppers would chatter and break when his face was being mercilessly pounded by the icy gale. A Santa with a bleeding mouth might be quite a shock for anyone possessing a telescope with an aperture of 70 mm or higher. Rosy cheeks were fully expected. Bloody shattered fangs, not so much. While some of the jabbas snapped Norman's boots into the clamps bolted to the sleigh floor, others tightly belted in his body and pushed his right arm into the iron brace. This gave the appearance that Norman was waving. Waving forever.

—

As the sleigh launched into the sky, the elves had the audacity to wave goodbye to him. They cheered as if he were a champion, as if they did not expect him to return from his trip an unrecognizable skeleton murdered by their own purply selves. As he rose, their figures became tinier and tinier, yet Norman could still see the celebratory dance which broke out in their ardent merriment. A devilish and floating Do-Si-Do.

—

Occasionally the reindeer, crafted entirely of hoarfrost, would sharply accelerate upward, climbing above the cloud rim. This was most likely done to avoid impact with obstacles and transmitted by slushy sonar inserted into their lifeless skulls. These motions jerked Norman blindly through long and terrifying veils of white. The seat pushing against his back, and his back muscles pushing against loosely connected organs inside his body. His eyes shut tightly, fully anticipating collision with a flock of wayward geese or the razor-sharp propellers of a helicopter. Perhaps he just waited to hear the piercing snap of the harness breaking off, as he and his jingling red coffin tumbled backward into the night sky. At other times, and again, without warning, the team would plummet downward on a 90-degree angle. Frightening though these dips were, screaming was out of the question, as during this zero-G airtime, Norman had to focus all his energy on remembering to breathe.

As the reindeer team straightened out once again, Norman saw the lights of cities below begin to lessen and then disappear altogether. He knew that vast carpet of blackness which now appeared beneath him was an ocean. Norman heard a rustle behind him. Unmistakably, a toy sack, shifting. Though his body was locked in place, Norman's head was not. It took more effort than expected to twist his face sideways and he could hear and feel a crackling on his neck where frost had accumulated. But now Norman was finally able to identify the source of the sound, and his heart thumped with life anew.

The lanky elf had freed itself from a sack and was now clambering over the back of the bench to reach him. Had Norman any tears left to cry he would have cried them. The elf immediately set to freeing him from his Yuletide bonds. First, he unstrapped the professor's belting and his arm from the bar. It was numb as hell, and there'd be a ruthless outbreak of pins and needles to follow, but at least, Norman acknowledged, he still had full function of the appendage. Now the elf moved to the floor, breaking the locks which held the boot clamps in place. Once unfettered, the elf freed each foot from its black rubber boot. Producing the red wool slipper socks like a magician pulling a dove from the air, he helped Norman slide his feet into them. The elf bore other surprising gifts, such as a warm and wonderful patchwork quilt adorned with fir trees. He placed it around Norman's shoulders. He also presented a small thermos steaming with hot mulled cider.

After gulping down half of the warm liquid, Norman placed both hands on the elf's shoulders, looked deeply into the creature's eyes, and nodded. Norman hoped the elf with the large cranium would understand how grateful he was for having saved his life, and the kinship he now felt for the creature. And when the professor was sure the lanky elf had received the message loud and clear, he let go.

The valiant little jabba assisted Norman in climbing out of the bench chair, motioning for him to move toward the back, among the sacks, perhaps to have more room up front to untie the reigns and regain control of the sleigh. Norman's will to take direction from his new hero was fervent, but his body could only navigate sluggishly, muscles sending irritating pain memorandums to the spine. At that moment, Norman felt his entire body being lifted. Just under the shoulders, vertically first, then horizontally, at the hands of a gentle, purple sumo wrestler. Elevated effortlessly, as if he wasn't stuffed tight with coconut rum balls and eggnog cheesecake.

———

The archipelago of the Lakshadweep Islands sits approximately 250 miles off the west coast of India. Had Pitti Island been inhabited, had it not been declared a tern sanctuary by the government in the 1960s, perhaps someone might have been lounging on the empty beach and spotted the Santa Claus, who tumbled out of a bank of clouds in the direction of Antarctica. At first, the Santa appeared as a giant red snowflake, butt and belly rotating, arms and legs flailing in all directions. But he quickly modified into more of a shuttlecock, body mass down, picking up speed as he screamed toward the Indian Ocean. To the surprise of the little jabba with the oversized cranium, Norman did not churn up the ice crystals under his feet to break his fall.

VIOLET'S BLOSSOMS

Josephine Queen

Petals drifting to the table, settling on the polished surface. The faint smell of decay, flowers resting in a vase a day too long. The water starting to discolor. A woman's voice, screaming—an angry cry, not scared. The vase lying on the floor, water puddling between tiles, flowers strewn, stems broken. A child crying.

———

THE BUS THUMPED through a pothole and Jessica woke. The dream licked along the edges of her mind. But the images dissolved quickly, like sherbet in warm water. Soon nothing remained but their aftertaste.

Jessica sat up and rubbed her face, unsure if she was exorcising the dregs of her nightmare or trying to crawl back into its depths.

Memory, Jessica thought. *Not a dream.* Not something her mind had created, but something it had recalled.

Rain tapped at the glass. The interior of the bus was hot and stifling. Condensation fogged the windows. The world beyond the glass hovered, suspended in mist.

Jessica wiped at the window with her sleeve. A town beckoned.

Shadow Hills.

Jessica recalled a phone conversation from three days earlier when she booked her room and transportation.

"The charter bus stops at Baskerville," the agent had said. "To get to Willow Falls and your hotel, you'll need to take a local bus."

Jessica sat up in the seat and unfolded a sheet of paper she'd been carrying. Her own handwriting was difficult to read, but she made out the scrawl enough to see she was close to where she needed to be. Willow Falls was just one mile distant from Shadow Hills. Much easier to get off here and walk rather than ride 10 miles to Baskerville and have to double-back.

She glanced out the window. The clouds looked heavy, but Jessica relished the thought of walking the mile to Willow Falls after being inert for the past 11 hours, rain or shine. It would be a relief to clear her mind of the webs of bad memories and half-remembered dreams.

The bus driver didn't see it that way.

"I can't let you out here, love," he said, a grimace stretched across his aged face. "Shadow Hills isn't a stop. Besides, there's no one here."

Jessica followed the driver's gaze. The town looked deserted, as if everyone had scattered as soon as the rain started, like cockroaches fleeing a flashlight beam.

"But I'm meeting someone in Willow Falls." Jessica held up her scrap of paper as evidence.

"This isn't a stop," the driver said. "I'll drop you at Baskerville and you can get the local from there."

Jessica squinted through the rain-streaked windshield.

"But you're stopped now," she noted. "And Baskerville is 10 miles in the wrong direction."

"Yes, but …" he started.

"Willow Falls is a mile away," Jessica persisted. "I can walk it from here."

"It's raining, love," the driver said, pointing at the darkening sky.

"Don't worry, I won't melt."

"Listen, love, you don't want to get out in Shadow Hills. Things happen here."

"What things?"

The driver shook his head. The door of the bus remained closed.

"Just ... bad things," he said, but he sounded tired and aware that he was losing the argument. A few passengers began to look annoyed by the delay.

"It's daylight," said Jessica. "What could possibly happen? Can't you just please open the door?"

Jessica was already down the steps. She hoisted her well-worn backpack onto her shoulder and turned to the driver. He looked at Jessica as if she were a bad taste that couldn't be rinsed away. It was the same look her mother had given her on countless occasions. Reluctantly, the driver pulled the lever and the folding doors opened. Jessica stepped out into the rain and watched as the bus slowly pulled away.

The main street was lined with storefronts, most of which were boarded up. Weeds grew through the cracks in the pavement. A cloud of failure drenched the town of Shadow Hills.

Perfect, her mother's voice spoke in her head. *You'll fit in well.*

Jessica felt as if she was being watched, the driver's warning playing with her nerves. She glanced nervously around, looking up and down the main drag, hoping to spot a warm, welcoming coffee shop or general store where she could charge her phone, get directions, grab a latte.

Sunday, it seemed, was not the day to conduct business in Shadow Hills. The rain fell heavier now and Jessica began to feel that departing the bus had been a mistake. Jessica was sure her mom would agree.

Her mom's voice—a grating, nasal, high-pitched tone that narrated so many of Jessica's nightmares—echoed in Jessica's head. *What did you expect? You're so bloody stupid, you've never made a good decision in your life!*

"Not true," Jessica said softly under her breath.

Jessica had made a great decision just two days ago, when she had finally walked away from her mother's stifling rules. Jessica touched her cheek lightly, still tender from being struck by her mother's hand.

"For the last time," she whispered, pressing ahead.

Jessica walked along the street, trying to stay beneath the ripped and moldering awnings. A large, washed-out cactus stood in a store window directly across from her, doubled over as if deflated.

Jessica sighed. She stood, shivering, beneath the meager shelter, unsure whether to wait for the rain to stop or to risk walking to Willow Falls in the downpour.

A flash of brightness in the grey caused Jessica to look across at the cactus store again. The window was now bursting with colorful flowers. Jessica frowned. The sign above the storefront announced, "Violet's Blossoms."

Jessica was drenched by the time she reached the door of the shop. She pushed open the door and stepped inside.

The humidity hit her first, then the scent of the flowers. It was overpowering, but not unpleasant.

———

They're sitting in the backyard. Her mother smiles at her from beneath the wide brim of a sunhat. Her face covered in shadow, unreadable. She smells the perfume of the peonies that grow like wildfire. Her mother's wine sits unopened between them on the blanket. Jessica tells herself that when she grows up, she won't drink alcohol. A child's promise to protect her older self.

———

The shop boasted roses, lilies, chrysanthemums, and many flowers Jessica didn't recognize. All were stunning in their vibrancy.

A woman, voice like honey, spoke from behind her. "Can I help you?"

Jessica jumped and turned. The woman was young and lovely. Sunflower blonde hair tucked messily into a ponytail. Hunter green eyes peered from beneath thick lashes.

"Oh … I'm sorry to bother you. I was caught in the storm. Do you have an outlet where I can charge my phone?"

"No." The woman smiled. "Can I help with anything else? Some flowers for a special person, perhaps?"

Jessica shook her head.

"Your mother, maybe?" The shopkeeper tilted her head. Jessica noted the fine lines around her mouth.

"My mother and I aren't … that is, she and I don't really get along," Jessica admitted.

"Such a shame," the woman said. "Mother-daughter relationships can be daunting, for sure."

The florist turned her back on Jessica and snipped at some errant leaves in a bouquet with a pair of clippers she pulled from the pocket of her apron.

Jessica glanced at the outlet next to the cash register. *Clearly she doesn't want to help me,* she thought, as she turned to leave.

"Do you love your mother?" the shopkeeper asked. Her back remained toward Jessica, who blanched at the question.

The shop was warm, much warmer than the bus had been. Jessica was suddenly aware of the rivulets of sweat running down the back of her neck.

"Well," she said, starting toward the door, "I should probably be going. Sorry to have wasted your time."

"Oh, don't leave," the merchant said and turned suddenly. Jessica stepped back, almost toppling a pile of pots stacked behind her. "It's such a nasty, gloomy day out there. At least wait out the rain inside."

Jessica wondered how she had mistaken the woman as young. Her hair was streaked with gray and the wrinkles around her mouth were deeply grooved.

"I'm Violet," the woman said, and offered her hand to Jessica. The skin on her liver-spotted hand felt paper thin and oddly cold given the temperature of the shop.

"I'm Jessica."

"Jess for short?" Violet asked.

"No," said Jessica. "I prefer *Jessica*."

"Right. Of course you do," Jessica noted the cynicism in Violet's tone and pursed her lips. The same tone her mother used with her. A mocking, passive-aggressive sound that always precluded a tantrum.

"Look, I just want to charge my phone," Jessica said. "Since I can't do that here, can you at least give me directions to Willow Falls?"

"To where?" Violet asked. She was occupied with arranging a flower vase. Jessica didn't notice the petals, which were brown at the edges, or the leaves that drooped, thirsty and dying, from the stems.

"Willow Falls," Jessica repeated.

"I've never heard of it dear." Violet started humming—a whispery, nasal tune.

"It's the next town over."

"No. The next town over is Bradbury."

"It's Willow Falls. I saw it on the map."

"I once had a daughter you know," Violet said. "She was a tart, too."

Jessica pulled her backpack further onto her shoulder. The door seemed a mile away. Violet now stood between her and the fresh air of the steadily darkening morning.

"Yes," Violet continued. "A tart. Daughters are tricky you know. Slippery things that twist your words and force your demons to the surface."

Violet smiled, brown teeth lined black gums, and not even the hyacinth and lilac could mask the stench of rot that seeped from her. Jessica took another step backward.

"What's your mother's favorite flower?" Violet asked. Her voice was hoarse, like a smoker's rasp.

"Peonies," Jessica said, trembling.

The stench in the shop was now malodorous, but underneath Jessica picked up the faint hint of her mother's perfume. There was a rustle as leaves and petals dropped to the floor. The smell of decay pushed through the perfume and Jessica wrinkled her nose.

Violet skittered across to Jessica and touched its tip.

"Funny little wrinkle-nosed chipmunk," she said. Jessica's heart lurched.

———

The hazy light of a spring morning. Jessica's mother lying on the couch, a puddle of red glimmering in the bottom of a wine glass. Her mother reaching over, touching the tip of Jessica's nose.

"Be a dear and pour Momma another glass."

Jessica standing, frozen, in the circle of light that dances on the living room rug. Her legs refusing to move. Standing in the sliver of time that shimmers between her mother's happy-buzzed and angry-drunk personas.

"Well, what are you waiting for? Funny little wrinkle-nosed skunk." The time passing like mercury, the light and mood changing.

"Pour me a glass of fucking wine you little shit."

———

"Mothers can be tricky. Daughters can be slippery," Violet said, in a whispery, sing-song voice. "Tarts and skunks and little shits. All of them need to be dealt with. Put out. Snipped off."

Violet clipped the rotting heads from a bouquet of roses. They fell to the floor. Violet watched with rheumy eyes wide and her mouth stretched in a humorless smile as they rolled, like the heads of small, desiccated animals.

Jessica backed toward the door. All around her, petals and leaves fell with an eerie whispering, decomposing into a rancid heap, then drying to a dust that caught on the wind as her hands finally found the knob and she flung open the door.

Her last glimpse of Violet was of the old crone collapsing to the floor in a pile of sagging skin and crumbling bones.

"Oh, God," Jessica whispered, staggering along through the rain, pace quickening with every beat of her heart.

The cactus in the window bowed down to Jessica as she ran, a mocking gesture to the daughters who lose their way and the mothers whose fingers they slip through, like sand through a sieve. Or grave dust to the wind.

—

The two o'clock bus thrummed into the center of Shadow Hills. The rain was slowing now, but the doors remained tightly closed.

A small hand wiped away the condensation that fogged up the glass of one of the many bus windows. A child's face peered out.

"Look, Mommy. Why is that lady running through the puddles?" The little girl, whose name was Rowan, watched as the young woman, backpack half off her shoulder, ran full pelt up the empty street. It was impossible to tell whether the woman was grinning or screaming silently.

Rowan's mother pulled her daughter away from the window.

"Don't stare darling, it's not polite."

"But she's not even looking at me," Rowan whispered. "She looked scared, Mommy."

Rowan's mother smiled and tapped her, not altogether gently, on the tip of her nose.

"My funny little wrinkle-nosed squirrel," she said. "Do as you're told."

Rowan turned back to the window and traced circles in the fog. Around and around, her finger went, drawing borders over the disappearing figure of the running woman.

THE DOGGONE GHOST

Bernie Brown

MARVIN TRUELOVE prided himself on his small feet. In fact, he fussed over every detail of his appearance. As head salesman in men's suits at Clark's Department Store, Marvin maintained a high standard, the likes to which he hoped his clientele would aspire.

Attention to detail also marked the care Marvin took within his department. Each morning, Marvin arrived early to ensure that each suit was properly buttoned. He also arranged stray suits, making certain that they all faced the same way on the rack and hung in ascending order of size. The morning of May 31 was no different. Marvin surveyed his sartorial kingdom with a pride seldom seen at the store.

Everything in men's suits stood ready and waiting for a banner sales day. Or did it?

Marvin's instincts twitched. Like beacons, his eyes scanned the sales floor. Not one speck of dust remained on the rack top displays. The shoes were polished and shone like mirrors. The socks display created a rainbow of color. Yet, despite this perfection, the thin hairs on the back of Marvin's slender neck stood at cautionary attention. Something was amiss.

Marvin checked the aisle that separated suits from athletic wear. He swiveled his neat little neck all the way down to outerwear and back to the changing rooms. Nothing unusual to be found.

He slowly walked up and down each aisle, checking between racks. All was well. At last he reached the aisle that led to the elevators. His inner alarm sounded loud and clear. Something was not quite right. In a moment he knew what it was.

"Oh, doggone it," Marvin said. This was the harshest expletive he would allow himself. "Doggone it. Doggone it. Doggone it." He ran a finger under his shirt collar, which suddenly felt too tight. It had happened again. Alarm mounting, he hurried to the display next to the elevator bays.

For the third time this year, the suit on the meticulously dressed mannequin—a double-breasted Yves Saint Laurent cotton-wool blend adorned with matching shirt and tie— had been replaced with something entirely inappropriate.

A bikini.

It was, in fact, the yellow polka dot variety popularized in that dreadful Brian Hyland song from Marvin's youth. The prankster had even stuffed several pairs of Calvin Klein socks—one of the most expensive lines—into the top to provide the mannequin a most unwelcome bustline. Marvin rushed to the storeroom to fetch the stepladder and undo the culprit's handiwork.

Marvin hastily redressed the mannequin. He was desperate to complete the task before the store opened and before Mr. Derleth, the tightly wound display manager, made his morning rounds. Marvin recalled the pranks from earlier in the year. In February, the mannequin had been dressed in a sequined thong, the type Marvin thought were completely inappropriate and ought to be declared illegal. In early April, it had been a skirted design.

"I'll bet the stock boy, Weaslie, is to blame," Marvin had complained to management following the second incident. "I scolded him for his sloppy unpacking, to which he told me to go to…" Marvin hesitated. "H-E double hockey sticks."

"Couldn't have been Weaslie. HR sacked him a week ago. You weren't the only one to complain about him."

Marvin couldn't imagine that anyone else would hold a grudge against him. He barely socialized with his coworkers. He ate his lunch in the breakroom, alone and away from the others, and abstained from caffeine, thus having no reason to socialize on a coffee break.

He had only ever quarreled with one other person at Clark's, though that was years ago, back when Marvin was a lowly stock boy. He disliked thinking about that. It had ended badly.

———

There. Finished. And with no time to spare. Marvin patted the elevator mannequin's expertly tied necktie, descended the stepladder, and hurried to return it to the stockroom.

Marvin hated the stockroom. Mysterious pipes and cables crisscrossed the cavernous ceiling. Metal lamps hung up there amidst all the apparatus. *Probably as dusty as the Sahara, Marvin thought. The doggone place is just plain spooky.*

A scraping sound emerged from behind a stack of boxes. Marvin shivered. He quickly hung the stepladder on its hook and returned to the comfort of the sales floor. *Clang!* He jumped and then turned to see that the ladder had fallen. *Must not have secured it.* He rehung it, this time making certain it was secure. Marvin rushed to leave. *Clang! Clatter!* The stepladder fell again. Marvin glanced over his shoulder.

"Tattle tale. Tattle tale. Hanging from a bull's tail." The voice came from behind those boxes and sounded vaguely familiar.

"Who's there?" Marvin called. His query was met with silence. *Oh, just leave the doggone ladder on the floor*, he thought. Perspiration gathered on his forehead. Marvin patted it with his neatly folded pocket square and quickly left the room.

—

Marvin nearly skidded to a halt by the elevator mannequin just as Mr. Derleth made his rounds. "I like this suit, Truelove. Might buy one for myself."

"You would look very distinguished in it, sir." Marvin hoped Mr. Derleth didn't notice that he was panting like a marathon runner. Stress made Marvin's heart beat irregularly, too. He took quinidine for arrhythmia.

—

The day passed without further incident. The store's Memorial Day sale didn't break any records, but a nice stack of receipts filled the accordion folder under the counter. At nine o'clock, Marvin checked the dressing rooms for merchandise, turned off the lights, and hoped that the elevator mannequin would remain properly dressed overnight.

Thoughts of the one man who might hold a grudge, might wish him ill, crept into Marvin's head. Marvin Truelove's mind was too tired to keep them out.

On several occasions in the early 1960s, during Marvin's years as a stock boy, he had encountered Harvey Busterd, the head salesman of men's suits at that time, behaving inappropriately with Ethel Fairwether of formal wear. On numerous occasions, Marvin had nearly tripped over them in the stockroom, their arms wrapped around each other like twin boa constrictors. Marvin recalled the time the staff elevator doors opened to reveal Busterd's disgustingly pimpled backside, Ms. Fairwether pressed against the wall. Then there was the time when he'd heard their passionate cries, moans, and grunts escape from one of the toilet stalls in the men's room. By late 1967, Marvin could take no more.

Marvin had reported his observations to the human resources manager—a most uncomfortable conversation. It happened that the brother of the HR manager was engaged to Ms. Fairwether. Word got around and both Fairwether and Busterd were let go "to pursue other opportunities."

But all that was so long ago, Marvin reasoned. *Water under the bridge, bygones being bygones, forgotten down memory lane. Or was it?*

Marvin suddenly recalled the long-forgotten handful of anonymous letters he'd received in the mail almost immediately following Busterd's termination. Each note, handwritten on Clark's Department Store stationery…

Tattle tale. Tattle tale. Hanging from a bull's tail.

A chill shot through Marvin's body as another realization surfaced from the recesses of his mind. *He's dead. Ms. Fairwether's fiancee shot and killed Busterd, point blank, only weeks after learning about the affair.*

At that moment, Marvin turned as a shadow caught his attention. He stared, dumbfounded, as the tweed three-piece suit he was about to rehang, a Martin Brothers design with suede elbow patches, puffed up as if Griffen himself, the ill-fated protagonist in H.G. Wells' *The Invisible Man*, had stepped into it. The chest expanded and the arms took shape, flexing to display the elbow patches. Soon after, those arms pushed aside the gabardine navy and the gray twill. The legs took form and the entire suit stood tall to stretch its tweedy arms. It had shape and bulk like a man, but was devoid of flesh. No bespectacled professor's head gave the garment dignity. No hands extended from the sleeves to sport an old school class ring. Only floor existed where brogues might have completed the look. Marvin stared, half-convinced he was dreaming, but the fluttering rhythm of his faulty heart convinced him otherwise.

The living garment approached Marvin and swatted his cheek, the wool scratchy and dry. Marvin backed away, staring, a fierce flush rising where he had been struck. He was struck again, harder this time but still little more than a slap. The force surprised Marvin and he stumbled backward and nearly fell to the floor. His weak heart responded. *Guh thump thumpitty thump guh thump thump.*

The suit lunged for Marvin. He turned and ran. He ran past the socks display, disrupting its orderly arrangement. He careened past sport coats, toppling the belts perched in the center of the rack. He rounded the corner into the stockroom. The dreaded stockroom. He imagined the dusty light fixtures laughing at him.

The suit, now quite the animated inanimate object, was at his heels, snatching at Marvin.

Marvin ducked in and out of the stacked boxes and discarded display racks. One rack tipped over with a resounding *clang*.

The suit continued its pursuit.

Marvin headed for the back stairs. He despised the back stairs, so littered with cigarette butts and dead insects. Carelessly, Marvin's toe struck the metal guard on the top step. The suit gave him a mighty push in the center of his back.

He tumbled for what seemed an eternity, bouncing.

Crack.

There went a rib.

He tumbled further.

His left arm popped out of its joint.

And further still.

One ankle folded under him. Excruciating pain shot up his leg and back. Marvin landed hard on his head, and a fearsome wrench shot through his neck. Now semi-conscious, Marvin wondered if the demonic suit would follow him down the stairs to finish the job it had started.

"Who…are you?" he managed, voice trembling.

Over the sound of his irregular heartbeat, Marvin heard a reply.

"Why, doggone it. I think he's dead. Tattle tale. Tattle tale. Hanging from a bull's tail."

Marvin winced at the high-pitched cackle that echoed in the stairwell as a shadow fell over him.

Marvin Truelove heard no more.

THE STUMPVILLE AFFAIR

James Goodridge

PROLOGUE

THE NEW CYCLE of a full autumn moon cast a cold, icy glow over August Mason's farm. Mason woke at 3:00 AM to the sound of his livestock. While the old farmer hated to venture out at this hour, he needed to find out why the hens were riled. Stepping out into the darkness, thoughts of Deacon Talbert—the local priest who had been recently murdered in the early morning hours—sent a chill through Mason's body as Wellington boots crunched atop the frosted grass as he walked to the barn.

"Something's got these hens worked up," said Mason, buttoning a denim peacoat. Brown earth mixed with manure caked his work boots as he rushed to the hen house. Hatless Mason cupped his eyes, avoiding the moonlight's glare, as its brightness made him nauseous.

Stumbling up to the hen house, Mason blindly felt around the inside wall, eventually locating a pair of dark tinted welders goggles, a memento from his days in the navy during the Great War. He slipped them over his cowlicked auburn hair.

"Now, what are you ladies cackling about ? Where's Mugsy?" Mason wondered aloud, inquiring about his king rooster. He suddenly felt a presence behind him. The hens fell silent in an almost human like terror. Stepping out of the hen house, Mason, a loner with no wife or children, turned around to face what was going to end his life.

The creature snatched at him as razor-sharp fangs bit into Mason's right arm, snapping it off at the elbow. Blood, bone, and muscle mass splattered about in the moonlight. Mason's lower arm sailed end over end into the air, finally landing atop the weathered house roof. As shock set in, August Mason howled in pain, body quivering. His cries reverberated into the village of Stumpville before trauma took him into eternal darkness.

Just before dawn, the day laborers Mason had hired approached in a dirty pickup. As the headlights grew nearer, the creature, which had been feasting upon the Mason's crimson and pink flesh, vanished into a nearby treeline. The hens, which had remained silent, resumed their frenzied cackle as Mugsy the rooster emerged from the crawlspace beneath the hen house.

1

Times were tough, even for occult detectives. Our clientele, those high society moneybags who hired Sue and I to chase ghosts or perform Tarot readings, had dried up as a reliable source of income. Contract work from the city's paranormal Office of Special Concerns had slowed because of budget cuts.

It was Tuesday, 12:35 AM. Dressed in stripped azure PJs and my red smoking jacket, I was in for the night. I sat behind my desk rolling around a nice-sized emerald from our stash on a desk blotter, wondering how much it might fetch. Off in the distance, a tugboat horn mewed deep on the Hudson River. At least the tug captain had work, unlike the occupants of Riverside Drive and 107th Street. A mug of hyssop tea on my desk curtailed my cravings as the silence of the room was suddenly interrupted.

I answered the phone on the first ring.

"Hello Kirkland," I said, aware that only Stuart Kirkland—the young "boy wonder" and head of the OSC—was the only person who would call me at this hour. "How goes it with you?"

"Hey, Madison, old pal. I'm peachy. Listen, I know that times are rough all over with this depression crud going on. so I figured you and Sue might be available for a job."

"Much appreciated," I said.

"Besides, this one's out of our jurisdiction."

"What's the affair? " I asked, intrigued.

"Upstate New York, Sullivan County. Village of Stumpville. The local sheriff, Kilroy Bertrand, has two unsolved murders which he believes were committed by … well … a werewolf."

"The sheriff's a real forward thinking fellow," I chuckled. "How did he decide to reach out to you?"

"You remember *The Life of a Lycan*?"

"The monograph you coauthored with Sue."

"That's right. She'd used the nom de plume *anonymous*. Bertrand read it. He thinks *anonymous* can solve their problem up there, because *anonymous* 'must be a werewolf to know so much,'" said Kirkland.

To me, that monograph was nothing but trouble. "So what's bub looking for, a Lycan to catch a Lycan?"

"I guess so, Madison. He sounds desperate."

"Yeah, but I'm also desperate for people *not* to know of Sue's propensities," I warned. "Okay, Kirkland, I'll ask Sue. She was under the weather last night and retired to bed a few hours ago. It's her call."

"Fair enough," Kirkland said.

"One question: The village of Stumpville. This a sundown town?"

Persons of mixed heritage like Sue (half native American and half Negro) and I (half Negro and half white) knew better than to work where we weren't wanted, money tight or no money tight.

"I'm ahead of you, Madison. Bertrand says it's an all-American, progressive town. They even have a few farms in the surrounding areas run by people of color," beamed Kirkland.

With that I pulled a yellow legal pad and pencil out of my desk drawer and took down the sheriff's information.

"I'll phone you later in the morning after I speak with Sue. Good morning, Kirkland."

"Good morning, Madison."

I pulled an Old Gold from my cigarette case, lit it with a magenta glow from my left-hand palm, and took a few quick puffs before snuffing it out in my tea mug. I left the smoky room and headed upstairs to Sue's apartment on the second floor, unlocking the door with her spare key.

"Sekhmet, sweetie, what you doing gal?"

Hanging upside down from the ceiling, Sue's pet cat, Sekhmet, meowed. Jet black fur tapered up to five silky black tentacles which held her in place while her forepaws played with a pink ball of yarn that trailed down to the floor among Sue's kaleidoscopic-colored harem pillows. Three innocent, copper-tinted feline eyes blinked at me.

"Come on, gal." I ordered, to which she plopped down on my shoulder, paws and tentacles secure in a piggyback ride to Sue's bedroom with me.

Sue lay sprawled out, face down in a black nightgown, throat rasping, and sniffled a sign of a cold in motion.

"Sue. Sue ? Wake up, love. I think I've got a paying affair for us if you're interested." I knelt by her bed and tapped her arm as Sekhmet hopped on my love's back, doing her best cat shimmy to break Sue's slumber."

"Madison Prescott Cavendish, do we have to talk now?" Sue asked, voice syrupy thanks to her cold.

On more than one occasion my Sue had been mistaken for Harlem starlet Fredi Washington, even being a stand in for the actress during a film shoot. But at this hour, rolling over to see me kneeling beside her and feeling Sekhmet resting atop her stomach, glamor was not on my beloved's mind.

"Job? Wha ... what is it? Where? I don't ... feel so good. How much does it pay?"

"It's upstate. Stumpville. I have to phone the local sheriff in the morning if we take it," I said.

"What's he want, a seance?" she sniffed.

"He ... um ... wants us to catch a werewolf."

Sue sat bolt upright.

"Come again?"

"A werewolf," I repeated.

Sue's pupils turned from black to hazel. Even her happy freckles, as I liked to call them, on her beautiful face were becoming inflammatory with anger.

"Seriously?" she asked.

"I kid you not. According to the lawman, this werewolf has already munched two people to death during a full moon. As I'm sure you know, the full moon is in cycle this week. I figure we go up there catch the creature, detain it until morning, then give it a one-way ticket out of town, no sore feelings. I know you were looking to celebrate Halloween, but we need the dough."

Sue frowned. "What if this werewolf is like me?"

My mind flashed back to 1914 and a nameless cosmic horror whose encounter in a lower Manhattan basement had changed our lives in ways we wouldn't have imagined possible.

"I guess we'll see what happens when we get to that bridge, my love. So, how about it?"

"Let me sleep on it, Maddy." Looking around but finding nothing upon which to wipe her runny nose, my Sue playfully ran it across on my pajama sleeve as Sekhmet's tentacle tapped displeasure on Sue's arm.

"Goodnight or good morning, dear," said Sue, rolling over to return to dreamland, with Sekhmet snuggled in her arms. I quietly retreated back downstairs to await her answer.

2

At eight o'clock sharp, Sue stepped into my apartment while I rested in peace. Rousing me awake, she looked fabulous in Halloween-colored attire. An orange bycoket with a black quill pointing out the top adorned her head, while her body was clothed in a black-belted orange sweater dress, black stockings, and semi-heels, all cloaked beneath a black trench coat. The overnight bag in her left hand meant I could phone the sheriff.

I dressed quickly; a gray tweed suit and white shirt matched by a gray fedora with black bowtie and wing tips.

Our first stop was across town to leave Sekhmet in the care of our friends, Zoltar the Magician and Elsa Cranberry, occult detective, both of whom were on idle time. Next we were off to Stumpville.

The concrete and asphalt of New York City in the midst of a depression faded into rural upstate New York, also in economic blues, as we cruised up the Hudson Valley in a dark cherry red 1929 Packard 640 Roadster. After a few hours I swung the Packard onto Stumpville's Lincoln Avenue, the town's main thoroughfare, where Halloween jack-o'-lanterns sat as festive sentinels at the base of lamp posts. Along the avenue, villagers went about their business, looking as if they had recently stepped out of a Norman Rockwell canvas. A few individuals of color confirmed what Kirkland had told me.

While Sue's nose continued its defiance, I parked the Packard in front of Sheriff Bertrand's office. The building was sandwiched between the Stumpville Post Office and an American Legion post that doubled as the mayor's office. I made an educated guess that Stumpville's population hovered around 400.

"Hey there, you must be Madison Cavendish and Seneca Sue. If not, I'll have to write you a ticket for parking in front of the sheriff's office in a spot reserved for official business," chuckled Sheriff Kilroy Bertrand, puffing on a pipe, hand outstretched to greet us as we stepped out of our automobile. He was a hearty soul, the kind you'd expect was born to work in law enforcement. Average height, rust-colored wavy hair under a dark felt hat, rosy cheeks, defiant light brown eyes that would rather squint than wear glasses, Bertrand wore a black suit covering a tieless plaid shirt. A badge on his lapel and a Smith and Wesson .38 holstered in a gun belt hanging at an angle below his pants belt were the only indications of Bertrand's occupation.

"Please, come inside. Glad you came," he said, as we entered into a drab pastel green atop Kelly green office with wooden courtroom-like barriers; benches on one side, front desk on the other. Bertrand ushered us into his office, past two deputies in khaki uniforms, each wearing surplus New York City police caps and engrossed in a game of chess. Dimly lit holding cells loomed in the back of the building.

"A few introductions are in order," Bertrand said, pointing to the three individuals seated at a table before us. "This is Mayor Douglas, Miss Katherine Livotti, and Doctor Neilson Zellner. They sort of make up the village council. We had a fourth council member, August Mason, but he was killed during the last cycle of the moon."

Sue, Bertrand, and I found empty seats. Mayor Douglas, a rotund man in an expensive navy pinstripe suit, had that old Roman Warren G. Harding look about him. Miss Livotti, a lanky woman with midnight dark hair saturated with pomade, looked tired in her royal blue dress. My impression was that she just wanted this problem to be over with. From the dagger-cold stare he issued, I suspected that the salt-and-pepper bearded Dr. Zellner, decked out in a blueish/gray double-breasted suit, didn't want us here. He wasted no time confirming my suspicion.

"I just want to" Zellner began, "for the record, voice my objection to this whole affair. It's a waste of village time and funds. Meaning no disrespect, what precisely do we know about these two hokum artists anyway?"

"Calm down, Neil," said Mayor Douglas. It was becoming obvious that this council wasn't exactly pleased with our presence. "We've already voted in favor of hiring Mr. Cavendish and his associate to help our village, and by Saxon that's what is going to be done!" The mayor's voice rose to a bellow.

"Please, everyone, let's relax. We are most certainly *not* hokum artists," sniffed Sue, to which the council lightly smiled (though I continued to receive icy looks). After giving them a redacted oral resume Sue asked. "How about letting us and the sheriff work out details and a plan in private."

The council nodded in agreement. Filing out of the sheriff's office, the good doctor seemed to be preoccupied in thought.

"Thank you," whispered Miss Livotti, finally perking up.

Bertrand retrieved a desk a map of the village and surrounding area. Two red pencil-marked 'Xs' denoted the recent killings and the time the bodies were found.

"Deacon Talbert died here," said Bertrand, pointing to a church in the south end of the village. "August Mason died here." An X marked his farm, just outside the east end of the village. "I feel the next attack will come in the north end," surmised Bertrand. I made a mental note that the sheriff's prediction seemed odd.

"Okay, sheriff," I said, "we'll need a pair of handcuffs, your map, and some type of anesthesia like diethyl ether."

"That's no problem, Mr. Cavendish. I'll have one of my men catch up to Dr. Zellner for the ether."

"We'll set to work around 11 tonight."

"I've set you up with accommodations. Drive further down Lincoln Avenue and you'll see the Doyle Hotel. Old Paddy Mullins will be behind the front desk, most likely napping. He'll have two rooms ready for you. I didn't know if you two were married or not and we don't do hot sheets up here." chuckled Bertrand. "Across the street is Carmella's Chop House. Put anything you order on Mayor Douglas' tab." Again Bertrand chuckled.

"We'll be sure to do that," Sue sniffed.

We soon headed down Lincoln Avenue. While stopped at a red light, I watched as a woman in a pea-green coat and tam with matching clutch bag chatted with a merchant in front of a sundry storefront. Next to her, a cherubic little girl, dressed as a smaller version of her mother, munched on a shiny scarlet apple. Me and the cornsilk ponytailed child made eye contact. I smiled and turned my green tinted sunglasses that protected my eyes and caught the light as it turned green. The little darling launched the apple into the car like she was on the mound at my beloved Polo Grounds, knocking my fedora off. Sue sat, too into her cold and her eyes closed, to notice. I felt an unexplained, strange vibe about this place, but couldn't understand why.

3

At Doyle's Hotel, we settled into our rooms to freshen up before crossing over to Carmella's Chop House.

"You're having steak. The iron will help with the cold," I explained.

"I'm really not hungry," Sue said.

"A rare steak for the lady. Hot water for me," I told the waitress, as she stood over our table.

"You only want water?" she asked.

"Yes. Hot water. For hyssop tea."

"We don't serve hyssop tea." The indignation was palpable.

"Then I suppose it's a good thing I brought my own."

The raven-haired waitress jotted down the order with Hellenic disdain and stepped away.

At the appointed hour, we got to work. This consisted of driving around the north side of the village, car windows rolled down so that Sue, despite her cold, might pick up the werewolf's scent.

Dawn finally arrived. Low on gas and with nothing to show from our night-long patrol but a shivering Sue, we returned to the Doyle Hotel where I made Sue a hot cup of hyssop tea with lemon.

"Get some rest, love. I'll be back to your room around 11:00 PM," I said, but the tea had already sent Seneca Sue SunMountain to Morpheus. Before turning in, I gassed up the Packard at a Sinclair station. The attendant seemed roiled when I asked him to fill the tank. We were a long way from New York City.

4

"I'm feeling better, sweetie," Sue smiled, as we started our second night of werewolf hunting, just one hour prior to Halloween Day. Similar to the night before, Sue wore only her trench coat, a pair of maroon house slippers, and rose-tinted glasses. This after so many ruined dresses resulting from spontaneous transformations. A change of clothes were in the back seat of the car. Cold gone, Sue enjoyed the night air for a few mundane hours.

"Ooh … woo!" Sue grabbed my right arm, suddenly. "Maddy!"

"What's wrong? You pick up a scent?" I braked the Packard to a stop.

"Yowzah! This village! I can smell so clearly now! This is … Maddy, we're in a village of werewolves! I can detect their scents all around me. Feel their blood pumping. One of their pack is sick."

"Well, hot damn this is a problem!" I exclaimed.

Indeed it was a problem, particularly for me, a living vampire. Historically, werewolves and vampires did not coexist well. This explained the vibe I felt earlier, not to mention the apple to my fedora.

"Quick, continue down the road a bit more until I say stop!" ordered Sue.

I drove along until her cue, stopping in front of a pleasant white-washed, two-story house. A well-picked pumpkin patch appeared to be the source of the jack-o'-lanterns lining Lincoln Avenue. Beyond a treeline nearly naked of leaves, a large shadowy figure emerged trudged toward the house. A little girl screamed from inside the house, its lights off and curtains drawn. The minty glow of the moon provided a spotlight for the final act of this affair.

A large, puss-dripping pink mass pushed its way out of one of the dark fur shoulders of the former Lycan. No longer a werewolf, it was in the process of sprouting a second head. The maw of the first head sagged, as if having suffered a stroke. One leg, devoid of fur, was rubbery black skin. Presently, the thing turned in our direction. Sue handed me her eyeglasses before leaving the Packard. She then slipped out of her trench coat, kicked off her slippers, and flicked her head to the moonlight. Knocked to the ground, on hands and knees screaming, her eyes bled as they turned from blackish red to bestial hazel. A grayish-magenta fur rose to cover my love. I issued a vampiric hiss, but before leaving the Packard, checked my Colt .45. Though loaded with silver bullets, I felt it would be lacking, so I removed my suit jacket. If I had to jump in, a vampire versus werewolf encounter would not be pretty. Doubtless it would be more deadly chaotic than a pier six longshoreman's brawl along the Hudson.

A horrid, grappling struggle ensued as Sue and the creature slammed into each other. Claws swiped, dirt flew, and pumpkins were crushed beneath the moon's stoic beam. I glanced quickly back at the house. The curtains, now pulled back, revealed the same apple-throwing little girl, mouth open in horror. A moment later, an unseen person snatched her away. Sue's claws were wrapped tightly around the creature's throat as she struggled to avoid its bite. A deadly tug o' war, which seemed to last forever, played out before my eyes. Sue gained the upper hand by lifting the creature off the ground before eviscerating it with a clawed swipe that dropped the were-thing to its knees. Steaming innards spilled out onto the frosty dark ground. Another swipe from Sue decapitated the beast. Its head spiralled like a football in search of a goalpost, blood misting into the night air. It landed beyond the treeline and rolled into the woods.

—

"Put that shotgun away, man!" I minced oath to the shadowy figure pointing the weapon at me from the second floor window of the house. "I need to use your phone to call Sheriff Bertrand. I also need a sheet to cover the body and water for my gal to wash up. We're working for the sheriff and the village council."

I clutched the were-thing's head, which I'd retrieved from the woods. Sue was bent over the back of the Packard, vomiting. Whomever held the gun likely didn't know that a full side of buckshot wouldn't kill me. After a quiescent few minutes, the door opened. A plump man wearing a nightshirt stood in the doorway.

"Names Culver," he said, handing me a sheet. "I already phoned the sheriff's office. Deputies Trusdale and Issacs are on their way. Your lady friend is welcome to come in and wash up."

In the distance, Sue began transforming back to her sparkling human form. I yanked the sheet from Culver, placed the were-thing's head in the pumpkin patch next to its torso, and covered the remains. I then helped a dazed Sue to the house, before waiting inside the Packard for the deputy sheriffs to arrive and for the sunrise to reveal who rested under the sheet. *Where*, I wondered, *is the good sheriff?*

5

"Help me understand something," I insisted, stepping up to Sheriff Bertrand's desk as he sat behind it with folded hands. "Since Stumpville is a village of werewolves, why didn't you take care of Miss Livotti's situation yourselves?"

Sue stood behind me, dressed from cloche hat to heels in black as if in mourning for Miss Livotti, whose vacant chair was next to Mayor Douglas and Dr. Zellner.

"Mr. Cavendish, I'm sorry," Bertrand said. "The people of this village have, for decades and from around the world, immigrated to Stumpville for a safe haven away from being butchered over lies and folklore. It's no accident that our village is named after Peter Stump of Germany and I myself am a descendant of the Bertrand family of France, so-called infamous names in Lycan history. Our ancestors settled in peace and harmony but with two rules: 1. Do not harm humans. 2. Lycan shall not kill Lycan."

"So, you made me, an outsider, her catspaw executioner?" Sue asked, trying to keep her anger in check.

"She made *you* her own executioner, Sue," said Dr. Zellner, choking back emotion. "I loved Kathy with all my heart. Earlier this year, she made the fatal mistake of picking and cooking wild mushrooms. The variety she picked, while nonpoisonous and delicious to humans, were poisonous to Lycans from souther Italy. She developed rabies. After farmer Mason's death, by her own volition, Kathy decided something had to be done. Sheriff Bertrand stayed with me all night so I wouldn't interfere. How I loved that woman."

Now shaking, Zellner eased into his lover's vacant chair, head in hands, sobbing.

"You loved her? Yet now, Sue, the love of my life, has become infected with that mushroom-triggered rabid illness!" I couldn't help but be tempted to make the doctor his own patient. "You could have told us!"

"Maddy, calm down, you lug. Whatever toxins were in me are long gone, or have you already forgotten the heaving incident behind the Packard? I'm as good as gold and you're still my man," said Sue, planting a kiss on my immortal cheek to the mayor and sheriff's blasphemous gawks. A vampire and a werewolf canoodling, indeed!

"On behalf of the village of Stumpville, I apologize for any duress. Katherine Livotti, rest her soul, is now at peace," said Mayor Douglas, speaking in an official tone as he handed us an envelope containing our wages.

"Madison and Sue," said Bertrand, as he escorted us out of his office to our Packard, a gray leather-bound book under his arm, "don't think what I'm going to give you is quid pro quo. It's from the heart. Tomorrow is All Saints' Day."

Sue and I stared curiously at Bertrand, unsure where he was headed.

"I'll be sending down to the city a truckload of venison meat on ice and apples. Seeing how times are hard down in 'Olde New York,' we in the village figured we could help out."

We nodded appreciatively.

"And look," the sheriff continued, "some nefarious person has placed two bottles of deer blood and a jug of fine applejack in your vehicle. We're still in prohibition, you know, so I hereby order you to drive the applejack out of city limits and enjoy it. Lastly, for you, Sue, a tome on Lycan heritage."

"*Histoire le Famille Bertrand*," Sue said, reading the title.

"I wish vampires had a village like this," I lamented.

"Corcosa," said Bertrand.

"What's that?" I asked.

"Corcosa, New York, up west near Buffalo. Them boys and gals up there like to work the midnight shift on the grain silos and elevators. We reached out to them, even challenged them to a game of baseball once, but they have yet to reply. Maybe they don't know the difference between a winged bat and a baseball bat," chuckled Bertrand.

Sue and I winced at the sheriff's attempt at humor.

After saying our goodbyes, Sue and I headed out of Stumpville. Halloween evening festively encroached. Children in costumes, and others as natural walking-upright wolf cubs, were already trick-or-treating. We were invited to stay for the grown-up activities, which included a Mardi Gras–style bash around midnight, a Lycan run in the surrounding woods, and an oration for Miss Livotti, but we were both missing Sekhmet and wondered what sort of feline mischief she'd been up to.

I stopped for a red light and saw Mrs. Culver with her apple-throwing daughter, Emma, dressed as a pirate and approaching us from Lincoln Avenue. The little darling released her mother's hand and ran up to the Packard. But instead of throwing another apple, she nervously handed me the candied variety before running back to mommy.

"Happy Halloween, Stumpville," I said, as we motored off back down to the Big Apple.

EPILOGUE

The sheriff was good to his word. We donated bags of apples and boxes of venison to folks in Harlem, The Bowery, and Hell's Kitchen. They needed it a lot more than we did.

In the years that followed, Sue and I made an annual October trek to Stumpville, each year growing more appreciative of its small-town charm and the glow of jack-o'-lanterns lined up along Lincoln Avenue.

TEACHER'S PETS

Linda Rumney

MONDAY MORNING. Mr. Wilkie braces himself for class. He stares at his own reflection in the men's washroom mirror. A few more grey hairs and a little patch of stubble he missed shaving earlier this morning. He needs an eye exam. He's noticed his eyesight fading for weeks now. Mr. Wilkie realizes it's nothing more than the effects of aging but he is disappointed all the same.

He straightens his tie, grape green, a poor match with his sky blue shirt, but who cares? He flattens the cowlick on his right side. The barber had not listened when he requested that it remain a little longer than on the left side so it would lie down, and now it stuck up as if he'd been sleeping on his face. A memory of his youth prickles at the back of Mr. Wilkie's neck, the awkwardness of his goofy hair, military style with a twist. That damned cowlick.

Mr. Nelson sits in a stall, a running commentary accompanying his various bodily sounds.

"I swear to God, if I have to eat one more freakin' cooking experiment I'll shoot myself. My wife ought to tell Cynthia we're not vegetarians. Who in the hell eats bulgur wheat anyway? Isn't that what aid agencies feed the poor in the Sudan? Jesus. I'm sorry … I should tell Cynthia myself, but it would only come out wrong, upset her."

"I have a class," offers Mr. Wilkie as he stealthily leaves the washroom.

"… her husband's not been dead five minutes," Mr. Nelson continues. "Carol, that's my wife, says the cooking class is therapeutic for Cynthia. Perhaps, but not for me. You know what I'm saying? Ah, god. You still there?"

Mr. Wilkie hears the noise from his class from the corridor. Twenty-eight teenagers who could care less about positive integers and will never appreciate the beauty of quadratic formula. He places a hand on the doorknob, takes a deep breath, and pushes into the room, back straight, eyes on his desk. The kids fall silent until some smart-ass starts to hum the theme tune to *Star Trek*, a running quip in reference to Mr. Wilkie's pointy ears. The kids erupt into sniggers and exchange fist bumps.

Mr. Wilkie has heard it all a million times and remains calm and quiet, waits for the hullaballoo to fizzle out.

"Turn to page 69."

More sniggering, but either the reference escapes Mr. Wilkie or he's heard it too many times to care. Without a beat, he turns to the blackboard and scratches out a math problem.

The kids fall silent again, rifling through textbook pages and protesting weakly. Peter, a Polish boy the size of a legendary linebacker, snoozes at the back of the classroom. Moonlighting for his father's trucking business keeps him up all night, so the classroom is but a resting place.

"Try to solve the problem in pairs and then we'll work through it." Mr. Wilkie checks the classroom clock against his wristwatch. He adjusts the time on the wristwatch. "You have 15 minutes."

The students huddle in pairs and hushed negotiations ensue. A hand goes up, Heather Givens.

"Sir, I don't have a teammate. Chloe isn't here ... again."

"Well now," Mr. Wilkie searches, "join Clare and Eve."

Heather pouts, gets up out of her chair and drags it, noisily, across the room, dumps her books on Eve's desk as Eve and Clare huddle closer together, rolling their eyes. Peter stirs at the back of the classroom but, thankfully, the disruption isn't enough to wake him.

Mr. Wilkie folds his arms across his chest, his tweed blazer a little tight across the shoulders. The leather patch on his left elbow has begun to pull at the stitching.

His mind wanders as he contemplates a trip to The Home Store over the weekend. He will purchase a few things for his guest arriving on Sunday, maybe a new tablecloth if he can find one, and some pretty plates or a centerpiece to make the visit fancier. He already has the menu thought out. Pork chops the way his mom used to make them, a little baked apple on the side, mashed potatoes and gravy, nothing that would break the bank.

Mr. Wilkie checks the clock, watches the second hand as it hits the 12.

"Okay. Who has an answer?"

———

Tuesday morning. Mr. Wilkie walks Skip, his aging Golden Retriever, before school. They take the same route every morning, a route that has become shorter as the dog's years have progressed and his rheumatoid arthritis has worsened. This morning Skip is slower than ever and Mr. Wilkie contemplates making the route shorter still or, perhaps, starting earlier. He scoops up Skips poop, inspects it for worms, and deposits it in a trashcan designated for animal waste amidst a frenzy of flies.

The bright morning has drawn out other dogwalkers, earlier than usual. On most mornings Mr. Wilkie has the quiet streets to himself. A blonde woman with a well-groomed, antiallergenic, nonshedding, crossbreed heads in his direction. Mr. Wilkie swiftly attaches Skip to his lead to avoid any canine interaction that might trigger a conversation. He avoids eye contact as the woman approaches. He chances enough of a glance at her to see that she is smiling, all lipstick and cheek implants.

"Well, hello there. Beautiful morning," she chirps.

Unable to ignore her, Mr. Wilkie nods and smiles pleasantly as they pass one another.

"Mr. Wilkie, isn't it?"

It's unavoidable, he must respond in case it's a parent. He doesn't recognize her, but after a while all parents look alike, sound alike, make the same jokes, and assume their kid is the brightest and best.

"Yes. Good morning. How are you?"

She laughs. "It's okay. You can drop the pretence. I'm not a parent. I'm Carol."

Mr. Wilkie stares blankly, strains to remember whom Carol might be.

"Ted's wife. Ted Nelson, from school."

The penny drops.

"Right. Yes, sorry. Ted, yes."

"Ted tells me you're single. No lady friend?"

Mr. Wilkie reels from the intimacy of the question, having only just met this up-to-now total stranger.

"Oh, don't mind me. I'm just a little Miss Busybody. I like to think it helps me look out for folks."

Mr. Wilkie does mind, but he tries hard not to show it.

"Well, it was nice to finally meet you. Ted talks about you all the time."

Carol throws her head back and expels a cackle that makes Mr. Wilkie's cowlick spring up like a startled cartoon cat's fur.

"I'd like to be a fly on the wall for those conversations."

"Oh no, it's all good."

Mr. Wilkie surprises himself with his social ability. Carol taps him on the arm with a well-manicured hand.

"I'm so glad we bumped into one another. I have a favor to ask."

Who the hell does she think she is? Mr. Wilkie wonders, a fixed smile on his face. She moves in closer and continues without taking a breath.

"We have a friend, Cynthia. She lost her husband last year and … well … we try to support her as much as possible, and God bless her, she's doing the best she can to overcome her loss. Cooking classes and whatnot. The thing is, she has been gifting us with the most delicious food from one of her classes, vegetarian cuisine, and Ted and I … as much as we look forward to these delights, simply don't always have time to appreciate them."

Mr. Wilkie knows she's lying. His smile starts to fade, anticipating her request.

"I was thinking it might work rather well for you both if, perhaps, she gave you the occasional dish."

"Oh, I don't …" Mr Wilkie checks his watch, seven minutes fast after the adjustment he made the day before.

"Okay, good. It's settled. I'll tell Cynthia."

Carol strides away before Mr. Wilkie has time to rebut.

"You don't know where I live," he calls after her.

"Oh, don't be silly," she laughs.

—

Wednesday morning. Mr. Wilkie walks Skip around the block. It is 5:00 AM. The street is quiet and only half-lit by an early-rising sun. No other dog or its owner walks the streets at this hour, which is exactly the way Mr. Wilkie likes it. He has enjoyed Skip getting older, less exposure to the risk of fellow dog lovers asking the statutory questions of others of their ilk. *How old? What's his name? Have you had him since he was a puppy? Is he a rescue?* Now 14, Skip came to him as a happy accident, as a puppy, yes. The woman in the pet store had told him, while he was collecting hay for Charlie, that someone had left Skip in the dumpster out back. He took to Skip straight away, the same color as Charlie, and hoped they would get along. At home, when he introduced him to Charlie, the chinchilla had seemed to take to Skip as well, much to Mr. Wilkie's delight.

Back at the house Mr. Wilkie feeds Skip and whispers a hello to Charlie, still hidden in his nesting box inside the large, tall cage in the living room.

"That wasn't so bad, eh Skip? I could get used to heading out that early every morning."

Skip chows down, a little deaf now, too, he only senses the one-way conversation and looks at Mr. Wilkie with a well-rehearsed gaze of acknowledgement that he knows will satisfy.

—

Thursday evening. Mr. Wilkie marks test papers. The neat piles stacked to match up with the checks on the blue gingham tablecloth. He does not add smiley faces or praise. His neat hand simply notes the answers as correct or incorrect with a uniform tick or cross and the total in the bottom right-hand corner. His final paper, perfectly timed, concludes with a knock at his door, the arrival of the take-out delivery boy.

When he swings the door open, wallet in hand, Mr. Wilke is surprised to find a shy, homely woman wielding a casserole dish.

"Mr. Wilkie, I presume," she jokes. "Stanley," she continues weakly, extending a hand.

Mr. Wilkie checks up and down the street for the delivery boy.

"I was expecting someone else."

"Oh, well. I'm not *really* Stanley, of course. I'm Cynthia."

"Oh?"

"Carol's neighbor. She said to come over. I brought you an eggplant cassoulet."

Mr. Wilkie eyes the dish cautiously, uncertain how to proceed. Cynthia extends the dish toward him, almost thrusting it into his belly, now embarrassed and close to tears. To Mr. Wilkie's relief the take-out delivery boy arrives and the distraction of exchanging payment for food lightens the tension and awkwardness of the moment.

Cynthia steps down from the porch and starts to back away.

"It will keep in the fridge for a couple of days. I can come back for the dish another time."

Skip appears at Mr. Wilkie's side and Cynthia seizes the opportunity for another attempt at conversation.

"Well now, who's this? Hello."

Skip waddles toward Cynthia to get a better look, completely blind in one eye. He sniffs at her for a moment. Mr. Wilkie, loaded with the casserole dish and the paper sack with his Kung Pao chicken and rice, shuffles on his feet, anxious to retreat inside.

"Skip."

"Ah, well, nice to meet you, Skip," Cynthia says, as she strokes the dog beneath the chin, the place he likes to be stroked best.

"It must be nice to have the company of a pet. My late husband …" Cynthia pauses, then begins to cry. "Oh dear, how embarrassing," she says. "I'm terribly sorry."

Mr. Wilkie surveys the street for a possible audience then resigns himself to inviting her in, lest the neighbors spot her and gossip ensues.

"Please, won't you come in for a moment?" he offers. "Just until you gather yourself."

"Thank you." Cynthia steps up onto the porch and pushes past Mr. Wilkie, a little cheered by the unintentional kindness.

Mr. Wilkie follows with the food and kicks the door closed with his left foot. He sets the food down atop the kitchen counter as Cynthia stands, awaiting the invitation to sit.

"Can I fetch you a glass of water?" he calls, through a 1950s-era serving hatch.

"No, thank you. I'll be alright."

When the invitation to sit fails to materialize, Cynthia wipes her face with a sleeve and takes a deep breath. She notices the cage.

"What's in there?"

Mr. Wilkie cranes his neck to look in the direction Cynthia is pointing, then appears beside her to offer her an explanation.

"That's Charlie. He's a chinchilla. He's nocturnal and very old."

"Sounds like me," Cynthia jokes. "I seem to come alive at night these days. Have trouble sleeping, you see."

Her pain is lost on Mr. Wilkie who eyes the paper sack hungrily.

"Well, you must be hungry," Cynthia says. "I should eat soon as well."

"Would you care for some?" The words escape from his mouth before he realizes it. "It's Chinese, from the new place at the end of …"

"Yes, I've seen it. I'll maybe just have a bite or two."

Mr. Wilkie moves his test papers and returns to the kitchen to divide the take-out between two small plates. He places one on the table and offers Cynthia a chair.

"Oh, that's far too much," she protests, but tucks in even before Mr. Wilkie joins her at the table.

"I didn't realize how hungry I was," Cynthia says, satiated.

"Isn't that always the way?" Mr. Wilkie comments, unsatisfied.

Cynthia twitters along like a dawn chorus as Mr. Wilkie pretends to listen. He thinks about Sunday and spending time with his guest and smiles to himself. Cynthia smiles back at him, mistaking this for an expression of pleasure, impressed that Mr. Wilkie is such a good listener.

Finally Mr. Wilkie pretends to suppress a yawn.

"Forgive me," he says, "I was up quite early this morning. It's been rather a long day."

"Of course, I don't know how you do it. I could never be a teacher. Any word on that missing student? Such a terrible business, her poor parents."

Mr. Wilkie shakes his head solemnly, searches for words of sympathy. "Chloe? No…"

"Well, I should let you get to bed."

Mr. Wilkie accompanies Cynthia to the door and she thanks him for a pleasant evening,

"I'm sorry for going on so," she adds "It's so nice to have someone to talk to."

She leans in unexpectedly and plants a light kiss on Mr. Wilkie's cheek. He catches a brief waft of lemon and pomegranates.

"Till next time."

"What?"

"I'll stop by for the dish over the weekend."

"Yes, yes," Mr. Wilkie says, narrowing the gap between himself and Cynthia with the door until she is gone.

—

Friday morning. Mr. Wilkie washes his hands at the men's washroom sink beside Mr. Nelson who is talking about his golf game in a language completely alien to Mr. Wilkie.

"It's a bit of a dream, but to play at St. Andrew's would be amazing. Too bad about the weather, though I guess that's why the course is so green, hah! And you, you dark horse, I never knew you had it in you."

"Excuse me?"

"You know. Cyn-thi-yah. She was on the phone this morning telling Carol how sweet you are. Sweet!"

"I … she showed up at my door with a stew or something. I think I made her cry so I invited her in."

"And?"

"And what? And nothing."

Mr. Nelson nudges Mr. Wilkie sharply in the ribs. "Hey, your secret's safe with me. Men of the world, right?" He smiles conspiratorially and makes an annoying clicking noise with his tongue in synch with a wink.

Mr. Wilkie raises an eyebrow. "I have a class to teach."

"Sure, buddy." Mr. Nelson slaps Mr. Wilkie on the back, tosses his paper towel in the trash, and walks away.

"Catch up with you later."

"Yes, later."

Mr. Wilkie surveys his face in the mirror. *"Men of the world?"*

———

Saturday morning. The weekend finally arrives. Mr. Wilkie holds a list of desired items in one hand and pushes the cart around the charity store with the other. Already resting in the cart is a nice china bowl which he plans to use for the salad. He sees a stack of complementary plates on the other side of the open shelf display and maneuvers around two Asian women in a heated dispute about a copper pan, both tugging at it fiercely. He places two of the plates in the cart and moves, quickly, away from the intensifying debate. The women wrestle to the ground and a child, sitting in a cart, wails hysterically. Amidst the commotion, Mr. Wilkie makes a dash for the checkout, pays with cash, and disappears from the store.

In the parking lot he sees Cynthia leaning into the trunk of her car. Without missing a beat, he jumps into his ancient Nissan and starts her up. He flips down the sun visor and startles at a sudden rap on the passenger-side window. He barely has time to think before Cynthia opens the door and squeezes into the seat beside him.

"Hi," she says, all smiles and warmth.

"Hello. How are you?"

"I'm good actually," she tells him, "I haven't felt this good since … well, I can hardly remember when."

"I'm very happy for you. That's … swell."

"Swell?" Cynthia laughs, "That's cute. I didn't think anyone used that word anymore."

Mr. Wilkie lets out a sigh and appears wounded.

"I'm not poking fun," she apologizes, misinterpreting annoyance for hurt.

"No, I'm sure," he asserts, irritated beyond words.

"Oh God, I've hurt your feelings, I'm so sorry. It's been such a long time since I've done anything like this."

"Like what?"

He doesn't have time for this. "Dating, of course."

Mr. Wilkie turns to Cynthia with a forced smile. He's prepared to do whatever it takes to get her out of his car so that he can carry on with his business.

"I'm not upset," he assures her. "I should apologize. I'm in rather a hurry, you see, and there was a disturbance in the store that set me back a bit."

"Oh dear." Cynthia reaches for the door handle. "I won't keep you."

She pushes the door open and clambers out. More than just a few pounds overweight, she is lacking in agility. Cynthia leans in as Mr. Wilkie starts to pull away.

"I'll come by and get that dish."

"Yes, fine." He steps on the gas and the door closes. Cynthia, an object in the rearview mirror that looks closer than it appears, fades.

—

Sunday morning. Mr. Wilkie awakes to Skip lapping his tongue over his face. He has grown accustomed to the early start to the day already, disproving the adage about old dogs and new tricks.

Mr. Wilkie pulls on a pair of casual pants and a pair of hushpuppies, too worn for school but still clinging to life. A dress shirt finishes his ensemble.

The morning walk is pleasant, if a little short due to Mr. Wilkie's eagerness to start the preparations for his guest. He cuts across Willow Avenue to Hope and through the back alley behind Gideon to bring them back to Albion and home. This early on a Sunday morning guarantees deserted streets, and this heightens Mr. Wilkie's excitement for the day ahead.

He feeds Skip and says hello to Charlie, as elusive as ever, hiding away in his nesting box. He takes a light breakfast of cereal and toast with strawberry preserves and washes the few dishes, a normal day in most respects except today he will have to ensure the air conditioning is set at its coldest and Charlie is removed to the spare bedroom so as not to feel too cold.

Mr. Wilkie drags the cage down the hall and throws a plaid blanket on it, the kind you might use for an impromptu beach picnic, not that lunch on the beach has ever been an option for Mr. Wilkie.

He scrapes the untouched eggplant cassoulet from the casserole dish into the garbage, washes and dries the dish, and places it on the porch should Cynthia happen by to collect it. He places a polite note in the dish:

> Delicious.
> Skip and I enjoyed it very much. Sorry I'm not home to thank you in person.
> Regards –

The note hints at him feeding the stew to his dog. A cunning plan to discourage any further offerings. *A clever one*, he thinks.

Mr. Wilkie turns on the oven, cores the apples, seasons the pork chops and peels the potatoes. Once the oven reaches the required temperature he throws in the tray of meat and apples, boils the potatoes, and prepares the instant gravy.

He showers and dresses in a clean, casual but smart shirt, unseasonably warm sweater and khaki pants, with pockets at the knee, a purchase from the outdoor recreation equipment store where he bought the extra-large cooler used by fishermen for transporting their catches.

The kitchen is arctic, save for the heat from the stove, which Mr. Wilkie hopes, will not alter the overall temperature and cause problems for his perfect lunch date. He sets the table for two and prepares the salad in the bowl bought from the charity store. The plates really do go well and he congratulates himself while admiring the arrangement. Skip wanders down the hall to the spare bedroom, the kitchen far to cool for his taste, and jumps up onto the bed, nestling into the comforter for warmth.

Mr. Wilkie unlocks the basement door, flicks on the light, and takes the stairs to the small space below the house. He retrieves a key from its hiding place under a half-empty can of Magnolia, eggshell finish paint, and unlocks the padlock on the chest freezer.

Cynthia arrives in her little red sports car, a gift to herself, the grieving widow, outside Mr. Wilkie's house. She has made a special effort today, her hair newly trimmed and her voluptuous figure squeezed into a summer frock, two sizes too small. She wears a pair of heels that her feet are attempting to escape from, swollen flesh oozing between the straps, as she hobbles, inelegantly onto the porch.

She sees the dish and frowns with disappointment. She smiles at the cute note and the sweetness of sharing with man's best friend.

"Well now, that is adorable," she sighs, and walks round the porch to peer into the house in the vain hope that he has not yet left, heels click-clacking in Morse code—
I'm here, it's me, yoo-hoo.

Mr. Wilkie hears the approaching footsteps from the basement and freezes to the spot, cursing uncharacteristically beneath his breath.

"Gosh, darn it."

He holds very still, suspending the large object he's semi-retrieved from the deepfreeze, half in and half out. Plastic wrap squeaks in his moist hands.

Cynthia taps on the spare bedroom window, spotting Skip on the bed.

"Skip, hello, Skip. Is your daddy still home?"

Skip, deaf and oblivious to Cynthia's presence, sleeps on.

"Skip. Skip!" Cynthia, concerned, calls out. "Oh dear, I hope he's alright." She moves to the back of the house and shoves her face up to the glass in the back door. She sees the table set for two and blushes with embarrassment.

"He's entertaining. He's having lunch with another woman."

Cynthia hammers on the door. "Mr. Wilkie, I know you're in there." She raises her nose to the air. "I can smell pork chops." She hammers again and leans in, listening for movement or lowered voices.

Mr. Wilkie stands firm, his hands start to feel the chill of the deepfreeze and the moisture has fastened them to the plastic. He wiggles his fingers loose and encourages the circulation back to regain feeling. His spine feels a twinge as he hangs over the freezer. Noiselessly he grimaces.

Cynthia persists. "Carol warned me about you. She said you were secretive. Well, don't think I'll be coming around again with any of my cooking, you … you creep." Unsatisfied by her own words, Cynthia offers a word of warning to Mr. Wilkie's lunch guest. "Watch out lady, you're probably not the only one."

She stomps round to the porch steps then peels off the heels, marked horrifically by the straps. She hurls the shoes at the sportscar then retrieves them and inspects the vehicle's bodywork for damage.

"Damn and blast it, Cynthia, he simply isn't worth it."

She throws the heels onto the passenger seat through the open window, forces her plump body behind the wheel, and starts the engine, revving the accelerator for dramatic effect. She throws the car into drive and speeds off down the street, startling a jogger on the sidewalk.

Mr. Wilkie waits for several moments until he hears the engine roar. He sighs with relief. "I thought she'd never leave," he whispers to the large object that emerges in his arms from the freezer.

He carries the object up to the kitchen and sits it at the dining table, frozen to fit perfectly on a dining chair.

"I hope the chops aren't spoiled," he says, pulling down the oven door, excited and back on track. "Ah, they're okay. Not burnt at all. That would be so embarrassing."

He drains the potatoes, adds lashings of butter and cream to the pan, and mashes them to a smooth mush. He boils the kettle and adds water to the instant gravy powder.

Mr. Wilkie serves the meat and potatoes onto two plates and places them on the dining table, one for him and one for Chloe, his chilled guest, who smiles coldly back at him.

IN DARKNESS, LOST

Bayne Northern

"SAMMY, I'M AFRAID! How did we get here?" Sean was quivering. Shaking with fear. Sammy pulled his brother toward him, hugging him tightly against his barrel-shaped body.

"I don't know how we got in here. But we will figure out how to get out! " he promised, trying to make his voice sound confident.

Sammy was the older of the two. He felt responsible for his little brother. Sammy could hear his mother's voice reverberating in his head, telling him to watch his little brother while she quickly scampered toward the ocean, her legs sinking into the wet sand, anchoring her as a big wave crested and broke, the foam rolling up the steep shoreline.

"It's dark in here!" Sean began sobbing.

"Don't be afraid! Let's treat it like an adventure! Let's try to figure out where we are, even though we can't see anything. We can still *feel* things. Tell me what you feel!"

Sean pushed himself out of Sammy's grasp. "Well, it's wet and sandy, just like where we were before."

"Excellent! Keep up the good work!" Sammy encouraged his little brother while he tried to orient himself. "It's is a lot wetter than where we were before. And a lot darker. I can't see a single ray of sunlight."

"I just bumped into something hard."

"Hard?"

"Yeah. Like a wall. It's cool to the touch."

Sean placed his body against the damp exterior, feeling around for some kind of opening–a possible way out. He followed the hard surface, cautiously creeping step by step, reaching up as high as he could go and then down into the wetness below, but he couldn't find any gap in the enclosure. The shell-like façade surrounded them.

Suddenly, a big gush of water poured into the wet and sandy space carrying little bits of seashells and pebbles, almost drowning both of them.

"I think I see something red in here. I'm scared! Did we get swallowed by a whale?" Sean's voice rose to a high crescendo. "Are we going to die, Sammy? Inside a fish? Mommy will never find us!"

Sean's little, rotund body began to shake violently as he sobbed. Small bubbles appeared around his mouth each time he exhaled.

"I don't think we're inside a big fish. Together, we'll find our way out! We are big and brave–brothers like no other!"

Their familiar war cry. They always chanted it when they competed in a sport, usually swim meets. Sammy excelled at the free-style crawl. Sean usually won the breaststroke.

"Brothers like no other! From the same mother!" Sean yelled from the other side.

That made Sammy laugh. He loved his little brother. They were truly bonded to one another. They looked alike, both sporting rounded bellies, shorter than most of their friends and all of the girls. But both agile swimmers. Excellent sandcastle builders. Adept at burrowing in the sand and burying one another within minutes.

Suddenly their dark, damp, sandy environment began to move. The whole area began to shake. Water swished from side to side. Sammy and Sean were pummeled by sharp seashells and small, smooth rocks. Strands of seaweed began to wrap around their legs, making it difficult to walk. Sammy pulled off the sticky green strands and quickly scrambled toward Sean, grabbing and holding him tight. His little brother started to wail. Whatever chamber they were in seemed to be swinging, first high to the right then down low and up again high to the left. The motion was making both of them nauseous. The lack of sight made them more susceptible to feeling movement. Then, the motion abruptly stopped. The water sloshed from side to side and then slowly settled down. More water was puddling on the right side, which made Sammy think they were situated on the side of a hill.

Unexpectedly, Sean and Sammy began tumbling around and around. Their environment spinning and turning upside down. The force of the water and sand poured from the bottom to the top, separating them. They could hear each other gurgling and gasping for air as they somersaulted in circles.

Just as abruptly as it started, the chaos stopped. They poked their heads out of the watery sandy mound. The brothers grabbed each other in delight, wrapping their five sets of legs around each other and squeezing tight. Their rounded exoskeletons clicked like castanets as they rolled back and forth in joy. Their feathery antennae intertwined. Their club-shaped eye stalks simultaneously rotated 360 degrees, first in one direction and then the other, happily scanning the familiar scene. They were back home. On the beach. They saw their mother frantically scurrying toward them. They both skittered backward to reach her.

Sammy and Sean looked up at the sky and saw a boy towering above them, running up from the ocean's edge, wildly swinging a bright-red, plastic bucket from side to side.

Further up the beach the boy's father stood waving his arms. "C'mon, son! Hurry up! We're gonna' grab a burger at Opie's for lunch!" When his son reached him, he fondly tousled his hair while he proudly praised him. "You're a good boy for letting your two sand crabs go!"

A shadow briefly covered Sammy and Sean as they watched the boy run away. Without warning, they both felt a sharp pinch, followed by the wind as it whipped though their antennae. Their five sets of legs were pinned against their exoskeletons. They were bewildered. They looked down and saw the ocean beneath them, the waves cresting and crashing onto shore. At the exact same moment, the sand crabs felt a sharp, shooting pain as their back shells cracked wide open. The seagull raised his beak up toward the sky, opened it wide, and gulped Sammy and Sean into its gullet.

The bird swooped down and around in a circular motion, returning to scan the shoreline for more tasty morsels.

MIRROR, MIRROR

Ellie Cooper

"I REALLY APPRECIATE the ride," he said. "Not many women would these days, but you can trust me."

I glanced at the stranger in my passenger seat. He was 15 years younger, but I'd been giddy as a teenager when I'd led him across the parking lot to my sensible, white Corolla. His shoulder-length blonde hair was different from the close-cropped hair of oppressive bosses, fathers and lovers. A tattoo wrapped his bicep like a pale green vine. His jeans were tucked into black lace-up Doc Martens. His left arm now dangled loose on the back of his seat just inches from me.

"You'll have to tell me if I need to make a turn or anything." I spoke too quickly, nervous now. The mirror's effect was wearing off like a short-acting drug. My hand swept the side of my face below my right cheekbone, an unconscious gesture or bad habit like a girl who bites her nails or picks at ugly scabs. I caught myself. Perhaps he didn't notice, but he was on my vulnerable side, where the scar hung, too dark for the rest of my face, dimpled like spackling the plastic surgeons forgot to smooth. It grew agitated when I had a fever, became embarrassed or stood beneath a bright light. I'd worked hard to be rid of it. I'd been to herbalists and faith healers, read books on

Native American remedies and Voodoo spells. Finally, I gave up and covered it with expensive French make-up. I glanced again at this stranger in my car. Another one of my mistakes I now feared.

I tried to remember my way back to the auction house, the red barn perched high on a hill, 30 miles outside of Austin. It had been postcard perfect earlier in the day, white picket fences and cattle grazing in fields of bluebonnets. The smell of fresh cut hay had been in the air when he'd asked for a ride. Now every time I asked, he said his sister's place was a little farther. A little farther down this dark, one-lane country road. I'd never find the highway. All I could do was stay between the white lines.

I glanced quickly in his direction. The night bathed him in shadows as it had when he'd stood in the soft glow of the building's lights while I searched for my car keys. I'd gone to the auction for the "Littles"—the out of print book, chipped plate, milk glass or knickknack—that would fill the shelves and empty spaces of my lonely existence. I'd found what I needed but had foolishly let it slip away.

His head had bobbled staccato like a little bird as he listened to Seattle Grunge over a pair of headphones.

"You didn't find anything you couldn't live without?" he said. I looked around, but he spoke to me.

He continued: "It was an okay auction. I only got some junk here for my sister who just got married." He pointed to a cardboard box at his feet.

And there I saw *it*—the mirror—propped along the side of his box.

I rushed forward and joined him in the shadows. I bent down and took the mirror without asking; I cradled it like a child with a found toy. "It was supposed to be in Box Number Six," I said. "I won the winning bid. Somebody must have switched it. It's mine—really." I was breathless and expected him to protest. I forgot my rule about not looking strange men in the eye. I only had 40 dollars left, but he might take a check. At flea markets and garage sales, I'd learned to haggle, offering half the asking price, hiding my interest in whatever caught my fancy. But it was too late for that. Too late to pretend *it* was unimportant. I rubbed the silver that was almost black with tarnish. I turned the mirror slightly and caught more of the light from the parking lot, and there I saw myself as I'd been when I first found it buried beneath hand-embroidered pillowcases and a pile of yellow curtains. I saw myself as I'd been a long time ago. As I'd been when Mother sat me on her lap and brushed my hair until my scalp tingled. As I'd been when she told me some day, I'd have a man to love me and children of my own. The safe, happy times before the cancer took Mother. Before Father had come into my room and started throwing my things, because I'd been late with dinner. Before her mirror broke and things turned bad. Before I'd run away and had the accident. A time when I was pretty.

"That a magic mirror, or what?" he asked.

His headphone rested around his neck, but his head still bobbled as if he listened to some internal music only he could hear. He wouldn't take my money. He gave me the mirror, because it meant something to me, he'd said. And now it lay face down on the back seat directly behind me. I could keep it near me always, in the car, if I wanted. I could look into it any time I felt bad or ugly. It had almost slipped away like a foolish old woman's lost youth and unfulfilled dreams, but he'd given it back to me. I'd been so grateful. He'd been waiting for a taxi he said, but I'd led him to my car instead.

"Yeah, I knew it was something special when I saw you inside like a little girl with her looking glass. You looked pretty from your good side. You use them fancy moisturizers and make-up they sell on TV? You work out?"

"What? You saw me?" I spoke without taking my eyes from the road, my voice barely a whisper.

"What's your name?"

"Lillian." Eyes still focused on the treacherous road.

"Pretty Lilly. I like that." He reached over and touched my scar, letting me feel the ragged edge of his fingernail. "Bad accident, or your old man slice you?"

No one besides Mother had ever called me Lilly. My face burned like the time I'd applied dilute Clorox on a cotton ball and tried to bleach the scar. I could feel it turn a deeper purple. I brushed his hand away like it was a gnat. Something was wrong. I'd taken a wrong turn from my cautious existence.

He leaned back in his seat. "Yeah, it's my lucky day you came along. I'm real surprised after them two girls that disappeared from these parts recently. You hear about them? Maybe just a little write-up in the paper. The one that worked nights at Walmart and then the other one. Margaret was a real looker, nice tits. Joanne something or other, had them big, chubby, cellulite thighs. You know what I mean? She didn't take care of herself like you. Both disappeared on their way home. A woman's got to be careful. You careful? Yeah, you looked real good from the side, talking to that fat, old counter woman."

He spoke of the auctioneer's wife who ran the snack bar. I'd rushed to her like a foolish child needing the wrong, righted—the hurt kissed away—after I'd won the winning bid and found the mirror missing from my box. "What kind of place is this, anyway? It was here!" I'd held up the cardboard box with the big black "six" written on its side.

The woman had been slow, lethargic and spoke with a sing-song German accent. She wasn't Mother. "Oh, I'm so sorry, dear," she'd said. "These things happen. Somebody fancies something in this box and something else in that box, but they don't want to pay for two boxes, so they put everything together in one box, and make sure they get the winning bid. It happens. We'll get you next time. You don't have to pay, dear."

I'd shoved the box at her. I'd whirled and run to the parking area where men loaded their Ford F150s and Suburbans with elaborate armoires, massive tables with legs carved like carnival balloons pinched and twisted into intricate shapes. My muscles ached from sitting on a hard church pew in the last row of the bidding area for hours waiting for my box to be auctioned.

I now remembered something else the auctioneer's wife had said as she'd passed out the bidding cards. *We have something for everyone.* Her words now stung. I glanced at the man beside me. He'd been waiting for something more than a taxi.

He still talked about the missing women. I tried to recall the one-inch pictures of the smiling, dark-haired women from the City-State section of the *Statesman*. Had their bodies been found? I breathed deeply to push the panic down, but it clawed against my chest like a wild animal trying to escape. The night was darker than the city nights I was used to. No streetlights or familiar landmarks to guide me home. There were no stores or stars. No place to turn around. I looked quickly to my left, and then quickly past him, to the other side. There was only a low sloping drainage ditch, the same as on my side. I knew there were mesquites, live oaks, prickly pears and life beyond, but all I could see was myself lying in   a field alone, insects crawling over my cold flesh. Only the headlights ahead to guide me.

"Pretty Lilly, slow down," he said. "You'll get us both killed."

I lifted my foot from the accelerator and watched the speedometer drop. Yes, slow down; you're not dead yet. Had he actually confessed? But the details, how could he know the intimacies of both women? Think, damnit. Think! Should I lie and say I knew Kenpo Karate, that my boyfriend was a detective and would hunt him down, or that I was HIV positive? I was exhausted and wanted it over. It would be, of course. Why else had he bragged, unless he knew I'd never repeat any of what he said. I didn't want to hear him, but he kept babbling. I wanted to give up, stop the car. I knew I couldn't outrun him, and after death, it wouldn't matter. But the torture could go on for hours, days, weeks. I wanted quick. But how? I glanced at him. It wouldn't be a quick death, one shot to the head. Perhaps I could hit a tree, maybe the crash would kill me. I studied him as he talked. Yes, he had the advantage, he was in control. I rubbed my scar. Find his Achilles' heel, everyone had theirs, I hoped. I forced my mouth open and tried to speak.

"Your sister," my voice broke. I tried again: "Your sister. You say she's recently married. Is she younger or older?" Get him away from the other women and back into my world. It was a slim chance. I wasn't a psychologist, but something I'd read came back to me. *Stand your ground. Don't go with him.* But it was too late for that!

He didn't answer, but he'd stopped his monologue. That's good. "Any kids," I asked. "Your sister?"

He was quiet now, but I heard the blood pound in my ears. Maybe I'd reached him.

A small hiccup sounded deep within him followed by childish laugher that choked his words. "Yeah, it works every time." His voice deepened. "Hell, after Ma saw me come out, she made sure there wouldn't be any more. She didn't even want me." His hand slapped the back of my seat.

I clung to the steering wheel. There was no sister, and I was in some unfathomable abyss. I'd taken him to a worse place, if that were possible. It was pointless, but I forced myself to continue. "I'm an only child, too. It was hard, very hard at times, but—"

"That so? Well, that makes us kind of related, don't it?"

"There were times—"

"You aren't wearing a ring, but that don't mean nothing now days, does it? You got a boyfriend, or you in between? I'll bet a fine lady like you has been married, what two-three times? He don't mind you out late like this? Hell, you didn't have to give me a ride, you know. I'd already given you your sorry, old mirror." He glanced towards the back seat.

His words were grievous, and he was back in control. I wanted to ignore him, but I wanted him to stop even more. "I liked you," I said. I knew it was a stupid thing to say as soon as the words slipped out. "I mean, I thought we could get to know one another, be friends, maybe."

"Yeah, I know lots of women like the way I look." I could see him flex his muscles and pump his chest; he tossed his lovely hair from his shoulders like Fabio on the cover of a romance novel.

Perhaps I could outlast him, keep him talking, keep driving until morning, wear him down. He'd grow tired eventually, wouldn't he? No one killed in the daylight, did they? Didn't all bad things happen in the dead of night? Mother's death, my accident. Perhaps we could find an all-night store and stop for a soda or beer. Maybe the clerk could hit the panic button around his neck or under the counter, before he—he what? Before they found my body days, weeks later after the insects had taken control. Work would call me at home tomorrow when I didn't show up and, eventually, the police. But by then, it'd be too late. For the first time all night, I thought of Harlan. Harlan who didn't want to marry me. Harlan whose relatives I'd never have to cook chicken cordon bleu or veal parmesan for again on Sundays. Harlan who only had to ask and I'd pack an overnight bag and hurry to his place. Harlan might not miss me for days. I thought of the bottle of Chardonnay on the back shelf of my refrigerator that I'd bought for him. I brushed my scar. *Who could ever love you?* it said.

My anger fueled me. "We could drive into town, any place, it wouldn't take that long, we could—"

"We'll party when we get to Doug's. It's just up ahead."

No, not two of them. "Listen, it's a nice night, we could catch the interstate, drive down to San Antonio, maybe keep going all the way to the coast. That'd be nice, wouldn't it?"

He didn't answer only stared out the window. How much time did I have? Ten minutes, maybe. I eased my foot from the accelerator, so he wouldn't notice. My thoughts raced like a train about to derail. I rubbed my scar again. *The mirror. Maybe, just maybe.*

"You know, it's my lucky day, too." I choked on the words but forced myself to continue.

"What?"

It was my turn to lie. "The mirror's turn of the century. There's an engraved mark on the back handle that's almost worn off. Fools at the auction don't know anything. You probably thought it was something sentimental. I wasn't going to say anything, but we're friends now, right?"

"Yeah, I thought it was valuable," he said. He seemed to cheer up and reached behind me for the mirror. He rubbed his big, strong hands over it, making me cringe. "How much you think it's worth?"

Suddenly, without thinking, I snapped on the interior light. "Why don't you take a look."

"Cool," he said. He held the mirror with one hand and fluffed out his beautiful hair with the other. I saw him better in the light. He was perfect. His skin flawless, his features Greek sculpture. His beauty—I bit down hard on my lip to stop the awful truth—he was everything I'd always wanted to be.

When I could, I turned to face him. He still stared at himself. Gently, I put pressure on the brake. He began to change chameleon-like before me; his shoulders sagged; his features softened. I stopped the car but kept it idling. I leaned carefully towards him to see what he saw, as he was a long time ago. The lovely, beautiful child. His hair even lighter like spun gold, his skin mother-of-pearl. But something was wrong. He was crying.

I wanted to ask why, but I had to act fast. The mirror's effect was temporary. "Look it's getting late, we have to hurry, get you home."

"Fuck you."

I recoiled as if his hand had struck me. "You want to get out and walk to your friend's house? Maybe you could spend the night?"

"Hurry up, don't stop, it's just up ahead. Hurry, please." He hadn't noticed we were already stopped. He began to cradle his left arm to his body. He shook. I could see the bone in his forearm was slightly bent at an angle as if it hadn't been set properly. My hand touched him lightly on the shoulder, but his good arm struck out at the empty air around him. When he'd quieted, I whispered. "What's wrong with your arm?"

"Uncle Doug."

I hit the gas hard and looked into the darkness for some sign of Uncle Doug, but all I saw in the headlights were rural mailboxes and a whiskey barrel with red verbenas. The houses were far between and set back from the road where screams in the night might go unheard.

"He's not really my uncle, but Ma told me to call him that," he said.

"Your Ma, where is she now?"

"The day after Ma died, he went out and got a woman. I could hear them laughing. Laughing at Ma and me. It wasn't even his house. It was mine, all mine."

"Go on," I said.

"He'd bring home women he'd pick up in bars or lonely waitresses at all night truck stops or sometimes runaways like Marie, but I knew what was going on."

"What?" I said. His silence worse than the truth.

"Marie was different. She liked me and was nice, fixed my breakfast sometimes, and I could talk to her. I can talk to you, too, can't I?"

I could feel his eyes on me. "Of course. You can tell me anything."

"Uncle Doug, he was mean and saw that Maria liked me better than him. She tried to warn me. She snuck into my room late one night, one eye all swollen shut. We've got to get out of here, she'd said. There was fear on her, I could smell it, you know what I mean?

His nostrils flared. "Like you," he said. He turned back to the window. "We threw my things into a backpack, but he came in."

"Your uncle?"

"He hurt her bad, taught her—her manners—he said, but he never touched me, at least, not my face. I got scars all over my body, you wanna' see? Afterwards, it got easier, he took care of me. We became a team. Him and Me. My looks lure them, you see. I'm sucker bait, and Uncle Doug reels them in. That's what he says. See women like me. Uncle Doug won't let me cut my hair. But they all asked for it, you know. I didn't force them to come with me like I didn't force you. Margaret was the first one that was strong and fought real hard. You gotta' separate yourself from them, Uncle Doug says. It's like a primitive tribe, they weren't family, not really human, but just ours for the taking—"

"No!" My voice reverberated in the confines of the small car. The mirror's effect was wearing off. "Look again, into the mirror, farther back before the pain. Try. What do you do for fun?" A dangerous question for this man, but the boy couldn't have been more than 12.

He looked at himself again. "Hang out." He wiped his nose with the back of his hand. "Play video games. At the Pack-N-Sack. Roy has a stack of *Playboys* he lets me look at in the storeroom. It's there, just ahead."

"What?"

"Pull over, now. Stop the car."

I almost missed it. The deserted, boarded up convenience store, totally dark. By the look of the sign, it had changed ownership at least once since the boy had known it. It wasn't what I'd expected, but I hit the brakes hard. My hand was on the door handle, but he opened his side first.

Please just go.

He turned towards me. "You got some quarters I can borrow?"

I emptied my change purse into his outstretched palm and gave him the two twenties I'd tried to give him earlier for the mirror. I watched him get out and adjust his headphones. I should have gone then, but I found myself in the quiet eye of a storm, my fear gone. We were joined, my knowledge, his deeds. He'd tried to run away also but had only gotten this far. His beauty had been corrupted and used against him. I ached for the boy. If my father had been worse, I might—but I stopped my thoughts. He turned back towards me. His handsome lips tightened into an ugly sneer. He was changing back. *No, just go, please.* He took a step towards my car, and instinct took over— his and mine. The automatic door locks clanged like prison gates, but he slapped the roof of my car, and I jumped as if his hand had finally found me. My foot hit the accelerator.

At a crossroad, I stopped. I couldn't get enough air; his stale boy's sweat permeated the car. Or was it my own smell? Should I call the sheriff and tell him I'd spent the evening with some nameless monster? I didn't know whether to turn left, right or continue on. I was lost in a web of dark county roads, not knowing where I'd been.

I looked for him in the shadows of my rear-view mirror. There was only darkness, but I knew he was out there waiting for me or someone else. Yes, and I knew he'd always be there. Waiting. My hand rubbed my scar again, and I thought of Mother, and then the auctioneer's wife. *We have something for everyone.* I rolled down my window and tossed the mirror far into the night, my tires crushing loose gravel like broken glass.

THE DARK AUGUR

Elizabeth Vegvary

THE WATER IS LUKEWARM, all the way through. Down to the bottom of the bathtub where her knuckles brush the smooth enamel, and back up to the top, open palms breaking the surface. The temperate consistency of it is comforting. Languidly she swirls clockwise and counterclockwise eddies with her hand as the bath fills. She has opened the faucet mid-way; tepid she thinks and then wonders if she knows precisely the meaning of the word.

The stoppered drain is a mouth she has closed. She is seated on the rim of the body of the tub, staring seeing and unseeing into and through the bathwater.

There are things she cannot remember—remembrance a river in her mind, the depths hazardous with the threat of submerged debris, carrying her forward never backward. She allows herself to recall standing very still on a narrow sand and gravel bank. The smell of sun-warmed fennel and bay and something else beneath that, sour and foretelling. The shadowy woods at her back, the sunlight ricocheting off the currents in front of her. The water moving too erratically ever to be a mirror. And she, the living girl, opening on the cusp, the sharpened curving arc of her that will cut away childhood.

Her flesh and bones recollect bare feet, gravel beneath tender soles, the chill of a cool stream wicking up her legs. Denim shorts and a simple cotton top, the warmth of the sun on the crown of her head.

A memory, like a body, surfaces from up out of the depths, it rolls then sinks again.

The small inlet is a swimming hole of neighborhood repute. You and Marissa know how to get there. You follow Peach Drive down to Rose Road where the construction on the new houses has churned up the meadow, transforming flowers into dirt. You keep walking, teaching yourselves how to whistle with a bent index finger and thumb in between your lips until the pavement ends and a footpath continues through the long and smelly weeds. Down a swale, up a swell and then back down into the trees. A forbidden hike.

Transients, your mother warns. Stay away.

Scumbags and dangerous, your father says. Don't let me catch you.

The neighborhood boys swim there from time to time, but most days the boys stay inside their houses, playing video games and drinking endless cans of soda. Neither of you has brothers. Marissa has an older sister; you have two younger.

The day it happens you have been sneaking down to the river for weeks. To kick off your Converses, wade upstream and back downstream and then lie your young bodies down on the August-hot gravel shore, eyes shaded with the backs of your hand. You talk about horses, wild and corralled.

It is the end of summer; you are both 12 years old, standing together in the water nearly up to your knees, practicing your whistles.

You don't hear him approach. He is not there, and then he is there. Standing at the tree line, the thin rocky border of land lying ragged and useless from the toes of his battered cowboy boots to where both of you are wading barefooted.

That's something to see, that is, he says.

The sound of his voice jerks your head up. You are not familiar with the taste of adrenaline or the experience of how fear skips through the body, a poorly thrown stone. Just an arm's reach away, Marissa's eyelids shutter then open. You hold her gaze, a lifeline.

Come on out of there, come on over here, he instructs.

You can only move your eyes. The knife is the scariest thing you have ever seen in your life. It glints in sharp sunbursts. It is long and tight in his fist. The world narrows to this man and his weapon. His sheer presence is a dark command completely foreign to you.

Now, one of you girls is going to do exactly what I tell you to do. He is wheedling. Or else you're both going to regret it sorely. I'm sorry to tell you that. But I am fully able to hurt you bad. So, be good girls and do what I say.

You begin to cry. Your shoulders are shaking.

And then what? Marissa asks, calling across to him.

Then what nothing. I'll go on that way, he points with the knife upstream, and you two go on back to your mammy's and pappy's where you belong. You ain't supposed to be out here, I'm betting. Isn't that right? This surely is not the place for two young girls. You even bleedin' yet?

He laughs, and the laughter becomes a cough and wracks through his torso until he puts his weaponless hand up inside his t-shirt and thumps at his chest. Never mind that. One of you is going to do a man a favor.

You think you might faint. You have once before, at the clinic. The nurse merely held up the hypodermic needle, and all the blood left your head, and you swayed forward into your mother's arms, darkness embracing you. It is the same feeling but where is your mother now.

What's the favor? asks Marissa and her voice is small but without a tremble. I'll do it if you promise you won't hurt us.

Marissa, don't, you tell her, but no sound comes out of your mouth.

It's okay, Marissa nods, a small movement barely perceptible. It'll be okay, she says.

That's right, Marissa, he says in an approving voice. I promise you. Come on up here now.

He waves her out of the water, and she obeys.

You reach out, but she is already stepping gingerly onto the rock and gravel, walking on the outer edges of her feet, towards him.

He points past Marissa and right at you with the tip of his knife, working the tongue of his belt through his buckle. Now you stay right where I can see you. I know secrets about you, girl. I'm looking at you and I know things.

What things, you whisper.

I'm going to tell them to you right after your friend here does me that favor. I'm watching you, girl. You'd run home by yourself, wouldn't you, now? Leave her here, huh.

Marissa is only slightly shorter than he is. You can see the shape of his body as though he is a corona outlining the shape of her body. He puts a hand on her shoulder, urges her down to her knees, and then puts his hand on the top of her head. He says something you can't hear.

You don't want to run; you want to sink to the bottom of the river, your skeleton becoming a perilous snag. Instead, you squat down in the water and it laps at your skin. You hug your legs tight and press your face into your knees to keep from seeing. Then you cover your ears with your wet hands.

He whistles for you. You look up. He has Marissa by her ponytail, pulling her to the edge of the water. He lets her loose with a shove and walks into the water, walks right up close to you.

He reaches for your shoulder and pulls you to your feet with fingers like claws. His lips are at your ear. You're going to drown your third born in the bathtub, he tells you. His breath reeks of something unknown. That's what I know about you.

He steps away from you, smiling through cracked lips, three of his front teeth are gone completely. His mouth is a black void. He shuts it and grins.

He turns and sweeps his arms wide; the knife calls all the daylight and swallows it down whole. Now you two get them sneakers and get ready to run, he tells you both. I might follow you. I might not. You better hope you girls are smart enough not to tell anyone nothing about this. I'll find you. I'll kill your mommas slow-like right in front of you, and you can't even imagine what I'll do to you then. He waits, tucks his thumbs into the belt loops of his trousers, the knife, a loosely dangling afterthought, in one sweat-grimed hand.

You reach down for your shoes, and then you run.

She dials off the water, wipes her hands dry on her jeans. She moves with deliberation. Out in the front room, her two oldest are on the sofa, snacking on a tube of Ritz Crackers. The baby is standing unsteady in the playpen, waving a gnawed cracker in her chubby fist.

You two behave now, she tells them. She leans down to lift her youngest up and out and onto her hip. The child melts into the motherly shape of her body, arms fast around her.

What are you doing, what are you doing? the two older girls sing-song in unison. Their attention glued to the television screen.

Just giving the baby a bath. Now hush.

THE SANDCASTLE

David W. Dutton

Martingale Beach – Summer 1925

THE RICKITY, WOODEN BRIDGE had not improved since last season and would likely get worse before it got better. It was the only access to the small, summer colony and would remain so until someone could talk the inhabitants into building a bridge strong enough to support the weight of vehicular traffic. Until then, summer residents housed their vehicles in a series of narrow, wooden garages on the mainland side of the canal. Everything needed for their summer habitation had to be carried across the footbridge.

Lewis Knight's left foot rested on the running board of the family Studebaker, which was parked in front of one of the garages. He turned and shouted to his wife. "Beatrice, are you sure we've unloaded everything?"

Beatrice tucked a strand of soft, brown hair under her wide, straw hat and smiled. "Yes, dear. I'm sure. If we've forgotten anything, we will just do without until Arthur can run across for it later."

"Okay. Adam, open the doors so that I can get the car in." Lewis pulled himself up into the driver's seat and started the big automobile.

Eight-year-old Adam Knight ran to the garage and wrestled with two heavy, wooden doors. Despite a lack of height and brawn, Adam succeeded in the job he'd been given, and his father carefully guided the dark green touring car inside the tight garage opening.

"Mother!"

Beatrice Knight turned in answer to her daughter's cry. "What is it, Jennie?"

"Clara simply refuses to cross the bridge. I can't do a thing with her."

Clara, the youngest of the Knight children, stood pouting at the foot of the steps leading up to the rickety, wooden bridge. "But Mommy, I'm afraid I'll fall through the cracks."

Beatrice started toward her daughter. "Nonsense, it's all in your head. Now just walk across like you would the red bridge in town."

"I won't!"

"That's enough out of you." Lewis Knight closed the garage doors and walked toward his family. "I'll carry you this once, but, from now on, you'll have to cross the bridge yourself."

Lewis hoisted Clara onto his shoulders and turned to survey the rest of his family. "Now, is everyone ready?"

Beatrice laughed and straightened her hat. "I think so. Arthur and James have already taken the water bottles across, so that should be about it. Jennie, have you got the other basket?"

"Yes, Mother. It's right here."

"Here come the Brewsters," said Adam, pointing toward the elegant Pierce-Arrow that had just turned onto the road. The sizeable, cobalt vehicle roared past as the two families waved to one another.

"Well, let's be off." Lewis Knight turned and climbed the few steps to the footbridge.

The sun shone brightly on the row of summer houses lining the sand. A light wind stirred the beach grass. The seagulls screeched overhead as the Knights picked their way across the bridge toward their cottage.

Lewis hadn't wanted to own the beach house, but Beatrice had insisted. It was so much better for the children than being cooped up in town all summer, she'd argued. So they had bought the small house, complete with a wide porch and three bedrooms that were just enough to accommodate everyone. It wasn't a bad place, and the selling price had been less than Lewis feared. With the exception of the Brewster house, which would have been an exception anywhere, the Knight's residence was typical of most of the beachfront summer cottages.

Anyway, they were here, and Lewis would enjoy it as much as the others once they were settled. He hated to pack and unpack after only traveling five miles from town. But that was the way Beatrice wanted it, and that was the way it had been.

—

Beatrice stood in the little kitchen, stacking provisions on the open shelves. She was happy with her summer home. It had been a hard-fought battle, but, in the end, she'd won. They had rented the little house for several years, and she thought that was simply a waste of money. Although they could have afforded to buy the house in the beginning, Lewis wouldn't support the idea. However, when he was finally promoted to bank president (and given a sizeable pay increase to accompany the title) there was no reason for further arguing. Beatrice was happy. She had her children, her house in town, the beach house, and money in the bank. What more could she want?

Beatrice turned from her task and looked out the narrow, kitchen window. The huge mass of the Brewster house obscured her view of the untamed stretch of beach. While it was quite a house, she did not envy Margaret Brewster. A house of that magnitude demanded significant upkeep and maintenance. Of course, the Brewsters, whose pockets were deep, regularly outsourced cleaning and repair tasks to locals, as they certainly didn't intend to spend the summer months performing home maintenance and upkeep.

The Brewsters and the Knights maintained a polite, nodding acquaintance. While they had summered side by side for the last five years, the families had little in common. Margaret and Edward Brewster were from Philadelphia. Beatrice imagined they were from one of the aristocratic families for which Philadelphia was famous, but that was only speculation on her part. The Brewsters only child, Chase, had graduated from college the previous year and then taken up employment at his father's firm. Beatrice had learned that Chase recently married and that the newlyweds were planning to spend the summer at Martingale Beach with his parents.

The slamming of the screened door woke Beatrice from her reverie. Clara and Jennie ran into the kitchen, tracking mud everywhere. They had been to the mud flats that bordered the canal. Unfortunately, this would be a regular occurrence throughout the summer. Beatrice could never understand the girls' fascination with getting covered in mud.

—

It was a tight squeeze getting the big Pierce Arrow into the narrow garage, but Edward Brewster finally maneuvered the car into place. The unloading had already been accomplished. It was now simply a matter of hauling everything to the house.

Edward handed his son two big baskets before picking up two more. "You know, it really is good to be back. I never knew I would miss it so much."

Chase shot his wife, Rebecca, a sarcastic grimace. "I don't see how anyone could miss that monstrosity." He motioned to the large, yellow and white convection with its ornate tower. It dripped gingerbread and confused the eye with its many gables and dormers.

"Chase, don't talk like that. After all, someday this will be yours." Margaret Brewster handed a suitcase to her daughter-in-law and then picked up another. "You young people simply don't appreciate everything we try to do for you." She paused and issued Rebecca a challenging stare. "What do *you* think of it?"

Rebecca hesitated and then smiled. "It's quite nice. I like it."

"I'm so glad that you do. Perhaps you can entice your husband to change his attitude about it. Edward and I worked tirelessly to create a retreat that our family could enjoy."

Edward shouldered another bag. "Well, I think that's everything." He took a deep breath and started across the bridge.

The two couples trudged through the sweltering heat while the gulls continued their chorus above. Rebecca kept glancing up at the huge house, oblivious of Margaret's eyes upon her. Chase slowed his pace until he was in stride with his wife.

"Don't mind Mother. She thinks this place is the end of the world."

Rebecca laughed. "It is."

"You don't mean you like it?"

Rebecca smiled in Chase's direction. "Heavens, no. I think it's perfectly horrible. Why ever did they build it?"

"*They* didn't. Mother did. Dad hates the place. So do I. As far as I'm concerned, it would make wonderful firewood."

"But your dad just said that he'd missed it."

"He only misses the beach. The house means nothing to him. He only built it to pacify her, to stop her from constantly complaining."

"I hope it'll never be that way with us."

Chase smiled. "It won't."

Edward unlocked the front door and threw it open to the sun. He stood aside to allow his family to enter. Margaret immediately walked through the foyer and into the big living room where she began to open the heavy draperies.

Chase leaned close and whispered to Rebecca. "What do you think of the interior so far?"

"It's a bit overwhelming."

Chase laughed. "Wait 'till you see the rest of it."

At his laugh, Margaret Brewster turned to glare at the couple.

Chase ignored her look. "Where are we sleeping?"

Margaret continued with her task. "You may have the front room. It will give you a view of the bay."

Chase picked up their bags and led Rebecca up the wide, walnut stairway. When they had disappeared, Margaret turned to her husband. He stood in the archway that separated the foyer from the drawing room. "Why he married that girl, I'll never know."

Edward looked at his wife and sighed. "Maybe he loved her."

"Edward, let's not be funny."

"Well, dear, some married people *do* love one another. It's not that unusual."

Margaret ignored her husband's comment and finished with the last of the draperies.

Edward watched his wife for a moment and then opened one of the French doors leading onto the wide porch. "I think I'll take a walk on the beach."

Margaret turned with glaring eyes. "Don't you dare. There's all this unpacking to be done."

Edward smiled and closed the door behind him.

———

Rebecca followed her husband down the long, dimly lit corridor. It was oppressively hot. The walls were dark, the carpeting was dark. The whole effect was claustrophobic. "Chase, why do you always disagree with your mother? It only makes her worse."

Chase ignored the question and threw open the door to their bedroom. "If you think the rest of the house is bad, wait until you see this."

Rebecca gasped. "Oh, my dear…it's…it's very, very red, isn't it?"

"Yes, well, technically it's gypsy rose. But yeah, it is indeed very, very red." Chase laughed again and pulled Rebecca close. "Do you think you can tolerate it here for the next few weeks?"

Rebecca kissed him softly on the lips. "With you, I can stand anything, even this ghastly mausoleum.

———

The sun was hot on Arthur Knight's back as he sat working in the sand. Even though he was 15, he still enjoyed building sandcastles. He'd been building them for as long as he could remember, and his father said that was one of the reasons Arthur hoped to be an architect.

"Arthur! Come on in now. It's time for dinner." Beatrice's voice traveled clearly through the thick summer air.

"I'm done. Come down and see it."

Beatrice stepped from the porch and picked her way across the sand. "I wondered what you were up to. We haven't seen you since lunch." She stopped and looked at her son while wiping her hands across her apron. "What have you built this time?"

Arthur looked up at her and smiled. "Don't you recognize it?"

Beatrice laughed. "Why…it's the Brewster place. Anyone would know it."

"Do you like it?"

"Oh, yes. You'll have to show it to your father. But why did you build it so close to the water? When the tide comes in, it'll be washed away."

"I know, but the sand here is wet and doesn't dry out like that further up the beach. You can work with it better."

"I see. Well, you'd best get cleaned up for supper. We're having the crabs that Jennie and Clara caught off the old jetty."

———

Little Adam rested his chin on the back of the sofa under the big window facing the bay. The waves came in long swells and were breaking softly against the sandy beach. The tide had turned about an hour before, while Adam and his family were eating dinner. Soon the waves would swirl around Arthur's sandcastle. Adam hated to see it go, because it was the best that he could remember Arthur having ever built. It looked exactly like the Brewster place, down to the tall, round tower that was so unusual. Maybe, with any luck, it would survive the onslaught of the tide, and Adam would be able to see it again tomorrow.

———

At the Brewster house, dinner had been nothing short of a trial. Chase was glad the meal was behind them, but he worried that the rest of their stay would be equally painful. Chase hoped that by spending time together, they would become more of a family. He knew his mother disapproved of his marriage, but he loved Rebecca and wanted his parents to do the same.

Now in their bedroom, Rebecca pulled back the heavy brocade bedspread accompanied with elegant silk sheets. She sat on the bed and tucked her filmy nightgown around her legs. "Well, that was fun."

Chase stood at the window and stared out at the bay. "Yeah, a real picnic."

Rebecca sighed and slid down under the sheet. "Maybe tomorrow will be better."

Chase laughed. "Do you really think so?"

"One can hope." She leaned back against the big feather pillow. "Your father's not so opinionated, but your mother, she's…"

"A real joy," Chase said. "Or rather, killjoy."

Rebecca was silent.

Chase continued to stare out the window. The wind was picking up, and the tide was rolling in. They could be in for a blow before morning. He sighed, closed the heavy drapes, and climbed into bed beside his wife. Chase ran his finger across Rebecca's brow and then kissed her smooth lips. "I love you, Rebecca Brewster."

Rebecca smiled. "And I love you."

—

Chase awoke with a start.

The wind howled, and the windows rattled in their frames. He lay there listening. There was no rain, only wind. The house shuddered with each violent gust. Above the assault, the sound of big waves pounded the beach. Never had they sounded so loud. Something was wrong.

His reverie was suddenly broken by his mother's scream. Chase jumped from the bed, waking his wife in the process.

Rebecca sat up and reached out to her husband. "Chase, what's the matter?"

"I…don't know." Chase left the room and headed for the staircase. His mother screamed again. "Mother! What's wrong?"

As Chase reached the top of the stair, water poured into the foyer, dissolving the front door in its path. It took him a moment to process the event. The door hadn't splintered. Hadn't collapsed. It had simply dissolved, leaving a trail of wet sand on the foyer floor.

Chase descended the stairs two at a time, but, before he could reach the bottom, the water had lapped over the first two steps, the newel post, and part of the railing. Only clumps of wet sand remained. Chase hesitated, grasping the baluster. "Mother! Where are you?"

Her voice was distant. "Here."

"*Where?*"

"The drawing room."

He looked toward the archway. In the dim light, Chase could barely see his mother. She stood on a chair, clinging to one of the ornate columns.

"Chase! *What's happening?*" Rebecca called from the top of the stairs.

Chase turned and looked up at his wife. "I don't know. Just…stay where you are." Chase returned his attention to his mother. "Mother, where's Father?"

Margaret Brewster sobbed. "Gone. He's…gone."

More water poured into the house, dissolving everything in its path. The front wall had almost disappeared, and there was no sign of the big front porch beyond. All that remained were lumps of sand being molded and scattered by the constant waves.

Chase began to panic. "What do you mean? Where's he gone?"

His mother sobbed again. "One moment he was on the porch. The next, gone."

Rebecca started down the stairs. "Chase?"

He gazed up at her. "No. Stay there!" Chase looked back at his mother. "Mother, stay where you are. I'll come to you."

Margaret Brewster began to cry.

Just as Chase was preparing to jump over the stair railing, a huge wave invaded what was left of the first floor.

The chair on which Chase's mother was standing dissolved, and she pitched, head long, into the swirling torrent. Chase stood in horror as his mother literally melted before his eyes. She didn't cry. Didn't make a sound. Chase gazed in disbelief for long seconds before recovering. He turned toward Rebecca.

"Rebecca, you need to get back to our room."

"Not until you come back up here with me."

Chase started to ascend the partially dissolved stairs. Another hungry wave assaulted the foyer, instantly washing away the remainder of the staircase. Chase reached out to Rebecca, but then the waves consumed him as well.

Rebecca screamed as the upper floors of the house collapsed. The waves greedily devoured walls, floors, and ceilings with equal hunger, until only a smooth, sandy surface remained.

—

The warm summer sun woke Adam Knight as it flooded his bedroom with morning light. Adam sat up in his narrow bed and rubbed both eyes. The boy had slept hard, not waking at all during the night.

Across the room, his brothers continued in their slumber, just lumps beneath the thin sheets. Adam stretched before swinging both feet over the side of the bed. He reached for his trousers and singlet and donned both. There was no need for hose or shoes. He was at the beach.

As quietly as possible, Adam padded down the hallway and then down the stairs. Silence filled the house. No one appeared to be awake.

Adam opened the door to the porch and stepped out into the warm, summer morning. For a moment, Adam paused, unsure what to do with this modicum of freedom. Then he remembered Arthur's sandcastle.

Without further hesitation, Adam jumped off the porch and sprinted toward the beach. The morning sun was already warm, and even at this early hour, the seagulls continued their never-ending cries. The sand felt moist and cool against his bare feet, but Adam knew that by noon, the sand would be hot and dry.

Adam skirted the clumps of beach grass and soon topped the last dune before the beach. There he paused and scanned the beach and the gentle waves breaking upon it. Nothing seemed out of the ordinary, but he saw no sign of Arthur's creation.

Slowly, Adam walked down the sloping sand, pondering where Arthur had built the castle. He combed the shoreline as far as he felt was feasible. There was no sign of the sandcastle–of *any* sandcastle–only smooth, white sand.

In the distance, Adam noticed an area where a lump of sand marred the surface. He supposed that might have been it, but had no way of knowing, and guessed it didn't much matter. The sandcastle was obviously gone, devoured by the hungry waves of the prior evening's tide.

Disappointed, Adam sighed as he turned back toward the family cottage. Then he stopped and stared. Something was different. Adam stared at his family's cottage and the expanse of sand that abutted it.

"What the heck?" Adam ran a hand through his thick hair. "Where's the Brewster place?"

The big house simply was not there. It had been there yesterday; of that he was certain. It had stood next to his family's modest cottage for as long as he could remember. Now, in its place stood a smooth mound of sand. Adam shook his head in disbelief.

Adam thought to himself for a moment and realized that maybe he was wrong. Maybe there'd never been a Brewster house. Perhaps the Brewster house, and its occupants, had been nothing more than a part of his eight-year-old imagination.

Overhead, the gulls circled in the sky, their screams echoing up and down the coast.

WAVES

Robin Hill-Page Glanden

"COME ON, MOMMY, take me to the beach," seven-year-old Dylan begged. "Daddy's busy and he can't take me. I wanna go make a sandcastle!"

Maggie sighed. She closed the romance novel she'd been reading and set down a half-empty glass of Pinot Blanc. "Dylan, you know I don't enjoy sitting on the beach. Wait until your dad's finished, then go with him."

"He said he's gonna be working for a really long time. By the time he's done it'll be dark. I wanna go *now!*"

Maggie stood up and walked to the kitchen where Gerald was halfway under the sink repairing a leaky pipe. Leaning down, Maggie asked, "How long you going to be?"

"A while," Gerald replied.

"Can you take Dylan down to the beach when you're done?"

"It'll be too late by the time I finish here. Why don't you take him this time? It's a nice day, not too hot. Can you please hand me the wrench?"

Maggie removed the pipe wrench from Gerald's toolbox and passed it to him. "All right, but we're not staying long."

"Okay Dylan," Maggie said, returning to the living room, "we'll go for a little while. Go get your sand pail and shovel and grab me a beach chair." Maggie downed the rest of her wine.

"And can we go to Dolle's and get a box of saltwater taffy?"

"Sure, Dylan. We can get some taffy."

"Yay!" Dylan ran off to the laundry room to fetch the beach gear.

Maggie walked back to the kitchen, retrieved a bottle of chilled Pinot Blanc out of the refrigerator, and filled her stainless steel travel mug. "We're going now, Gerald. Be back soon."

"Okeydoke," Gerald mumbled from under the sink.

Maggie placed her novel in a tote bag, then grabbed a flowered silk scarf from the hallway table and tied it over her dark brown curls. She walked with Dylan the three blocks from their house down to the beach at the far north end of the Rehoboth boardwalk. It was early September. The tourist season was over and school was about to resume. The beach was deserted, much to Maggie's delight. She settled down in the weathered beach chair just shy of the shoreline as Dylan started happily digging in the wet sand. Maggie watched her young son as he laid the foundation for a sandcastle. Designing and building sandcastles was Dylan's passion. Gerald said their son would grow up to be an architect.

The sun was warm and a gentle breeze came off the ocean as high tide arrived. Maggie typically didn't like to sit on the beach, baking in the sun. Her fair complexion burned easily. Gerald, on the other hand, enjoyed the beach and always took Dylan along. But today's weather was pleasant and comfortable. Maggie unscrewed the lid of her travel mug and sipped the cool wine before starting Chapter 5 of her novel.

Despite the steamy romance that was developing between the book's main characters, Maggie began to feel drowsy. The warm sun, the cool breeze, the sound of the ocean—all of these elements were like a lullaby. Maggie's eyes grew heavy.

—

She woke with a start. Maggie felt disoriented and she had no idea how long she had been asleep. The sun hid behind clouds and the wind had picked up. Maggie looked to her right where Dylan had been crafting his sandcastle. The base of the castle and his shovel were there, but Dylan was gone. A moment later, she heard Dylan's voice. Looking up, she saw him out in the ocean with his head barely above water and crying for help. Maggie panicked. She jumped up, but stood paralyzed with terror. Maggie felt helpless—she didn't know how to swim. She looked around frantically, but there was no lifeguard presence during the offseason. There was no one in sight.

Dylan screamed again before he vanished beneath a huge wave.

Suddenly, Gerald sprinted past Maggie, stripping off his shirt and kicking off both shoes. He dove into the water and started swimming toward the spot where Dylan went under.

Maggie watched as Gerald dove beneath the water, resurfaced, then dove again. He continued to search for his son. Finally, he resurfaced with Dylan and started swimming toward the shore. Gerald gently placed Dylan on the sand and started examining him as Maggie ran toward them.

"Is he all right?" she asked, breathlessly.

Gerald didn't answer. His face was tense as he applied chest compressions. Maggie started to cry, sobs shaking her body.

She turned at the sound of distant sirens. *Someone must have seen what happened and phoned 9-1-1*, she thought, relieved that help was so close now. Two paramedics appeared and tended to Dylan. Gerald fell back onto the sand, soaking wet and exhausted. The paramedics placed Dylan on a stretcher.

"I'll ride in the ambulance," Gerald barked at Maggie. "You get the truck and meet us at the hospital."

"I want to go with you," Maggie cried.

Teeth clenched, Gerald ordered, "Get the truck and follow us."

He ran to catch up with the paramedics. Moments later, the emergency vehicle sped off toward the hospital. Trembling with fear, Maggie quickly gathered up their belongings and ran back to the house.

———

She arrived at the emergency room 20 minutes later and found Gerald sitting in a chair, staring out the window.

"Is he okay?" Maggie asked.

"I don't know," Gerald replied, his voice shaking. "They're working on him now. Good thing I came down to tell you that I finished working. You were gone a long time."

Maggie put her arm around Gerald's shoulders, "I'm so sorry. I fell asleep. I should have been watching him."

Gerald looked up at Maggie. His eyes flashed with an anger she had never seen before. "That's right. You *should* have been watching him. Dammit Maggie, you had one thing to do– watch our son. Were you drinking? I really don't have to ask, do I? Of course you were."

Double doors opened and an ER doctor emerged. With a weary expression, he approached the couple and shook his head sadly. "I'm terribly sorry. We did everything possible, but we lost him." The seasoned physician paused for a moment, knowing his words would take time to sink in. "You can go inside and see your boy in a few minutes.   I'll have a nurse come get you. Again, I'm so very sorry."

Maggie burst into tears and collapsed into a chair as the doctor walked away. Gerald stood frozen. Finally, he turned to Maggie.

"You never wanted a child. Even after Dylan was born––you didn't want him. You always treated him more like a bother, an annoyance."

Maggie gasped at the accusations. "That's not true, Gerald. No, it's true that I didn't really want children, not at first, but you wanted a son. And I wanted to give you a son because I love you. I always loved Dylan."

"Well, we no longer *have* a son," Gerald said. "So you should be happy now."

"That's a terrible thing to say, Gerald," Maggie said, tearfully.

The couple stood silently for several minutes until a nurse escorted them into a room where Dylan lay lifeless on a cold, metal table. A white sheet covered his entire body. The nurse gently pulled the sheet down to reveal the boy's face. Maggie sobbed quietly. Gerald's eyes filled with tears.

When they returned to the waiting area, Gerald grabbed the truck keys from Maggie. Without a word, he turned and headed for the parking lot. Maggie followed behind him.

—

Maggie walked alone toward the water. It was cloudy and cold for early September. The chilly wind blew Maggie's long, white hair back away from her face. She stopped, scanning the ocean, remembering that afternoon exactly 15 years ago. She continued down toward the water's edge, moving slowly. The arthritis in her left knee was bothering her more than usual. As the waves washed over her feet, soaking her bedroom slippers, Maggie heard a voice call out.

"Hey, Mom, what are you doing?"

Maggie turned and gasped at the sight of her tall, handsome son. "Dylan, you're here!"

Dylan grinned. "Of course I'm here. Where else would I be? What are you doing in the water? You don't like the beach. And look, your slippers are all sandy and wet. Dad has breakfast ready. Blueberry pancakes—our favorite. Come on now. Let's walk back to the house."

"Your Dad made breakfast?"

"Yeah. He makes breakfast every Saturday morning. You know that. He even made that French roast coffee you like so much."

Maggie walked toward Dylan slowly, confused. "Dylan, you drowned 15 years ago. And your father, two weeks later he followed you into the sea. Told me he was going out for a walk, but never returned. His body washed up onshore the next day. You were both gone. I was left alone. So alone."

"Mom, did you have that dream again?" Dylan asked. "Like I've suggested before, maybe you should see a therapist for a while. You keep having that same horrible dream."

"Yes. Yes, I guess I *did* have that dream again."

Dylan motioned for Maggie to follow him. "Come on, Mom, let's go home."

Maggie turned and headed toward the boardwalk. Back at the house, as she walked up the steps to the kitchen, she felt a familiar sense of dread.

Her chest tightened. She felt lightheaded. She braced herself, opened the door, and stepped into the kitchen. The stove was cold. The coffee pot was empty. The breakfast table was set with one plate, one glass, one coffee mug, one spoon, one knife, one fork.

Maggie leaned wearily against the kitchen counter. Another day, starting like so many others for the past 15 years. She sighed, then took the coffee carafe to the sink and filled it with water. She scooped French roast into the filter, then poured the water into the machine's reservoir. She pressed the ON button. The machine sputtered into action. As Maggie watched the dark liquid trickle down into the carafe, tears streamed down her cheeks.

She was so tired of it all. Dylan and Gerald would not let her follow them into the sea. She had tried and tried, but they refused to let her go. Maggie poured a cup of coffee and added half and half. The first sip in the morning always tasted so good. Something about a steaming hot cup of coffee always brought Maggie a cozy, comforted feeling. *Caffeine always seems to clear the cobwebs out of my head*, she thought. Maggie sipped slowly, savoring the beverage. She cupped both hands around the mug to feel its warmth. Usually she would go back for a second cup, but this time when she finished, she rinsed the cup and set it in the sink. Then she went to a drawer in the pantry and, after rummaging around a bit, retrieved a small box. She took a deep breath, sat down at the kitchen table, and struck a match. Maggie touched the flame to the edge of the flowered linen tablecloth. The fire spread quickly to an adjacent stack of newspapers. For the first time in so long, Maggie felt a wave of calm wash over her, followed by a quiet sense of blessed peace.

MR. GIBB'S BANNER YEAR

Heidi J. Lobecker

THE KIDS OF STONEBRIDGE High School always crossed their fingers when they were in the gym. On the wall, a commemorative photograph of Old Coach Rogers glared at them. The iron-grey eyes gave Kevin, the quarterback for the Wildcats, tingles on the back of his neck.

"What's he so mad at?" asked the new kid.

"He's pissed we keep losing," said Kev. "His teams won a ton of championships, and now we just suck."

"Chin up, Kevin," Principal Dugan said. "This year, we'll turn it around. I'm recruiting a different coach. One with a history of winning."

When the final bell rang, Principal Dugan watched the stream of people leave. He fingered an old black whistle in his pocket. He was looking for the new algebra teacher, Mr. Gibb; Mr. Gibb, with his lame handshake and doormat demeanor.

Ahhh, there he is, Principal Dugan recognized Mr. Gibb's shuffling gait. *That man's shadow is more noticeable than* he *is.*

"Take a walk with me," Principal Dugan said, grabbing Mr. Gibb by the elbow.

"Oh, okay," shrugged Mr. Gibb.

The two men stood in the gym, the photograph of Coach Rogers hanging on the wall before them. The rank smell of old sweat and damp concrete hung heavy in the air. High above them, keeping company with the dust motes, hung 11 Division 1 State Championship banners—the glory years of the legendary Coach Rogers. The faded red and black banners proved that though Rogers' memory lived on, his winning streak was as neglected as the academic standards of Stonebridge High.

Coach Rogers was an old-school, hawk-faced man. Twenty years ago, when Coach spoke, his team listened. Even now, his picture commanded respect; in it, he wore his starched shirt, black tie, horn-rimmed glasses, and a tweed hat.

"That man gave his life for football," said Principal Dugan.

Mr. Gibb mumbled a response and chewed his lower lip. His dull brown eyes glanced at the picture.

Principal Dugan resigned himself to talking to this dud of a man. He told the story of Coach Rogers with the reverence it deserved:

"We were playing the Vikings. Our men played sloppy, and old Coach Rogers couldn't stand sloppy. He was pacing the sidelines. He had just given Ed 'The Tank' #19 the next play, and then he grabbed his right arm in pain. He knelt on the grass, just six minutes into the game, he collapsed on the 50-yard line. Ed quickly called a time-out and rushed to Coach Rogers' side. No heartbeat. He died on the field right on the sidelines."

"Huh," said Mr. Gibb; he tried to look suitably solemn.

"He worked here right up until the day he died," said Principal Dugan. "That field is sacred ground." He gave Mr. Gibb a side-eye.

"Sacred ground," repeated Mr. Gibb dully. Mr. Gibb figured he'd die playing video games on his couch—his default pastime as he limped along through life. He hoped his neighbors found him before his dog, Woody, ate his face. He wouldn't mind if that happened though; Woody was the only one ever really happy to see him.

Prompted by the jock-talk, Mr. Gibb said the burliest thing he could think of: "I used to be a volunteer referee for my nephew's football team." It sounded suitably athletic.

"Oh? You got family around here?" asked Principal Dugan.

"Not really. My sister's in the Army. They're in Germany now."

Principal Dugan, always grasping and pawing at things, nodded eagerly. His big hands pushed Mr. Gibb forward into a dim office, situated at the back of the locker rooms.

"Yes, yes. I saw you were a referee on your resume," the principal said. "You have so much potential. We need a football coach to start summer training for the Wildcats right away." White globs of spit gathered at the edges of his mouth in his excitement.

"C-coach?" Mr. Gibb stammered, wanting to avoid responsibility. "Oh no, no. I couldn't do that."

"It's an extra $4,500 for the season," said Principal Dugan.

"Okay, then show me where to sit," said Mr. Gibb.

Principal Dugan gestured to the cracked black Naugahyde covered chair, patched with duct tape. It went with the worn, metal desk, at least 20 years old.

"Great, great," Principal Dugan said. "I'll leave you to it. Good luck." He hung the black whistle around Mr. Gibb's neck. He quickly closed the door and scuttled off before Mr. Gibb could change his mind.

Principal Dugan walked out of the empty locker room. The dingy pipes leaked slow drip-drip-drips into shallow puddles on the floor. The walls curled off strips of gray-green paint. The lockers hung half-open like dark mouths, squeaking on rusted hinges.

Principal Dugan stood in the gym, stared at Coach Rogers' picture and yelled, "He's perfect."

Eleven red and black banners fluttered in a foul breeze.

———

Even in the full heat of a sweltering August, in the small office, Mr. Gibb felt a cold chill. To distract himself from the decay, Mr. Gibb did a quick search for "How to coach high school football."

The gym stink condensed around him. Five minutes into reading "15 Tips for a Great Practice," Mr. Gibb felt lightheaded. Needing fresh air, he got up to open the door. It was stuck, the rotting frame had swollen in the humidity. He grabbed and pulled at the doorknob with wet, sweaty hands. The dull metal slipped around in his slick palms. The door would not open.

Heavy pressure in the air pushed down on his shoulders. He could not move. A fast wind slammed musty, mildewed playbooks off the shelves. The same wind, full of fists, pounded him BAM BAM BAM like players going after a running back at the bottom of a fumble pile.

He desperately tried the door again; his hands scrabbling and clawing at the knob. A foul breath pressed his face.

Frantic to get the door open, he pushed and pushed, harder and harder. The air was dense and dank; the room shrunk around him.

He pushed, pushed, PUSHED!

The door slammed open. Breath uneven and short, he stumbled out. A helmet, full of teen boy smell, flew at Mr. Gibb's head. A solid hit. Mr. Gibb fell to the ground, unconscious.

When he came to, he was dragging a two-man sled from under the bleachers. He looked over, and three more sleds were lined up on the 10-yard line. His shirt was sweatier and smellier than it had ever been in his whole life. He realized he'd moved 300 pounds of steel all on his own. He stood a little taller and smoothed his hair down across his balding scalp. He tried jogging as he went by the 50-yard line, blowing the old whistle as he went by.

That night Woody sniffed and snorted at him when he arrived home. The dog wouldn't come near him until he showered twice, in extra hot water. He had to scrub hard to remove the fusty tang that clung to his body.

———

It was one month before school, and the Wildcat's prowled the field.

"All right, boys, let's get started." Mr. Gibb tried to command the team's attention, but they were much more invested in the phones they'd snuck onto the field.

"Boys," he tried again, "I need you to listen!"

"He's just a boring old dude with bad B.O.," said Kev, the quarterback, when the team gathered in the huddle. "I wanna work on my short game. Let's do some passing drills."

Tired of insta-lurking the cheerleaders, the boys practiced a shotgun formation they knew. The ball arced hard and fast in the crisp fall air. Mr. Gibb, ineffectual as ever, decided to end practice early when the dank smell rushed at him again.

He sniffed the rot in the air and raised his puffy arms to wave it off, but he was too slow to stop the speeding football. The ball headed right for his temple; that pigskin missile didn't miss.

Mr. Gibb woke up, smelling of jock itch, sitting at Coach Rogers' beat-up metal desk. Mr. Gibb's weak fingers pushed at the sore on his head. The boys were finishing up their showers, and he caught bits of their conversations.

"Mr. Gibb was no joke at practice today. He ran our asses off."

"That way he showed us how to use a sideline to stop a running back was cool."

"Never would've guessed that old guy had it in him."

The side of Mr. Gibb's head may have been tender, but for the first time in his life, his ego was full. His ego liked that.

He stared at a well-worn red leather notebook placed in the middle of the desk.

Written in the careful cursive, and proper penmanship taught by nuns, were years of experience from Coach Rogers on what turns a boy into a football player. Mr. Gibb read what it took to transform an unfocused 100-pound 15-year-old into an All-State quarterback. How football makes men of boys. How to form those men into a team. How to lead that team to three consecutive state championships.

Mr. Gibb pulled out his own notebook and began to take notes. Notes on making sure the boys took care of their uniforms. Notes on how to build a team and how to let the boys find their strengths and weaknesses.

He learned the importance of knowing how to act. He had a new game plan for practice. He would start by reminding the boys they needed to be class acts—not only playing football the right way but how they conducted themselves.

Mr. Gibb absorbed page after page of sage, straightforward advice; the old Coach whispered in his ear.

After he read a good 50 pages, Mr. Gibb gathered up his things and said goodbye to the boys. He noticed the team covered their noses when they talked to him, breathed through their mouths to avoid his scent. A nasty draft followed him out, pushed between his shoulder blades, making sure he stood up straight.

He stopped at the store, loaded up on odor-removing laundry detergent, room spray, and extra strength deodorant.

He picked up extra treats for Woody; they were having a hard time living together. When he got home this night, his usually happy mutt rumbled and barked at him, circling around him with his hackles raised aggressively. Woody spent the night in the garage.

Practices started going well, and when the Wildcats walked in the hall of the math wing, they growled, low and deep. The normally apathetic students yelled hallway chants, "Go Cats, Fight Cats!" Stonebridge hadn't shown this much school spirit in decades. Principal Dugan proudly told his wife the whole place sounded like the tiger house at the zoo.

At the front of his class, Mr. Gibb stood tall. He now wore button-down shirts and a black tie. The snarling, howling boys were his. Showing up, digging deep. They came by to get him, to escort him to practice, the coach of their team. They didn't walk too close though.

They wanted more of his wisdom, more offensive plays, more strategies like using a short passing game to move down the field successfully. He liked the respect. He could never remember what he did to deserve it.

"Glad to see you brought back the short passing game," said Principal Duggan, "that's how we would win, back in the day."

Mr. Gibb nodded. The attention and compliments felt good; he hung onto them to cover the taste of vomit in his mouth. He had pine tree fresheners in the pockets of his blazer to hide his rotten egg smell. No one dared say it to his face, but he heard the offensive line call him "Dank Stank."

He was sad when Woody ran away, his only real friend in life. He put up LOST DOG signs in the neighborhood, featuring a big picture of the brown and white mutt.

He spent a week looking for him. But in his heart of hearts, he knew Woody needed to be gone. Woody's frantic whining, pawing, and clawing at the door to get out, get out, GET OUT when feeding time came just about broke Mr. Gibb. At that moment, he wished he could run away with Woody, leave his sour milk stink back at the school. When Mr. Gibb inhaled deep to relax, he smelled what had permeated his soul.

—

It was early September, and the new and improved Wildcats were ready for their first game of the season. Mr. Gibb led them onto the field, looking especially dapper in a new tweed hat.

"How do you feel we'll do against the Vikings?" Principal Dugan asked. He was standing upwind from Mr. Gibb.

"Our team is ready. They know what to do. It's time we beat this team."

"Look what I found," Principal Dugan said. He held up a #19 football jersey, properly cared for just like Coach had taught him. "I remember climbing into my pads for my first game and putting on this jersey. It was the best and worst day of my life. The first day I played in a game. The day you died."

Coach looked at the jersey and nodded to the man before him. He'd always had high hopes for Ed "The Tank" Dugan; it was no surprise the boy had grown up to become principal of Stonebridge High School.

"Good to have you back, Coach," said Principal Dugan.

Coach walked towards the 50-yard line, his iron-grey eyes focused on his players, his mind already planning his next move.

"Good to be back," said Coach.

He blew the old black whistle hard and sure. The players turned to him, fired up, ready to go.

"Best make room for another banner, Ed," yelled Coach over his shoulder to Dugan. "After all, there are no championships when you're dead."

THE SEA CEMETERY

Andrea Goyan

IZMIR TO LESBOS, port to port, 30 minutes," Lonan said, fastening the clips on Raahel's life vest. "Like we never leave land."

"Only we do," Raahel said.

"It's safe, my love." Lonan tucked the ends of Raahel's scarf beneath her straps.

"Aegean's full of the restless dead," she said and made the sign of the cross.

Her husband laughed. "You sound like an old woman." He held her head between his hands. "The dead are dead."

She twisted from his hold. "It isn't safe."

"Which is why I bought you this," Lonan said, as he lifted Yawsep from where the baby lay supported inside the donut hole of a foam safety ring. Lonan held his son aloft, high over his head. "You're as big as a two-year-old in your vest! You are."

Yawsep giggled, and for a few seconds, Raahel too laughed and forgot where they were, what the night held in store. The moment ended when a burly man approached Lonan and leaned in close. Raahel watched as her husband slipped the man a handful of lira, saw the sneer that painted the man's face before he swaggered away. Lonan motioned her over to the boat. There was a tightness in her chest. A life's savings poured into this one hope.

"Our time," Lonan said. Raahel took his hand, and together they waded knee-deep to the waiting boat. "We die if we stay."

Raahel nodded, and Lonan, holding Yawsep in one arm, helped her onto the boat with his other. The rubbery surface was wet, and her feet sought purchase on the wobbly deck. She took Yawsep from Lonan's arms so he could board. He helped her to the rounded edge of the vessel where she took the seat she knew he'd paid extra to procure.

"Hold here," Lonan said. He grabbed the thin rope that ran along the perimeter of the craft.

Raahel nodded, even though she knew what he asked of her was impossible. She needed both arms to hold Yawsep. He was too small to hold himself and too big to secure with just one arm, especially in his life vest. Lonan nestled the safety ring beneath the crooks of her knees. As other passengers clambered aboard, the boat tipped and shook. Raahel gasped.

Lonan kissed her head. "I'm going to the back of the boat to help."

Raahel grabbed his hand. "Stay."

"The sooner everyone boards, the sooner we arrive in our new home."

Raahel knew he was right, and she released her hold, though the thought of Lonan leaving her side nearly paralyzed her.

The moon was bright enough to see the other travelers as they crowded on deck, but Raahel wished she couldn't. They looked like washed-out remnants of human beings lacking any flush of life, and Raahel wondered if their hearts still beat inside their chests. Hers did. It pounded so hard she felt it in her throat and temples, in the arms that cradled Yawsep. The refugees crammed aboard until every square inch was occupied by anxious families. Raahel reached an arm over the edge and wetted the tips of her fingers. The boat sat much lower in the water than when she'd first stepped onto the vessel. A horde of strangers stood over Raahel, their feet stepping on her toes. Raahel felt like every breath she took was another person's exhalation, containing all their fears on top of her own. She struggled to take even shallow breaths. Worse, Lonan was stuck on the other side of the dinghy. He waved to her, his face largely a silhouette in the darkness. She clenched her jaw and looked the other way.

The band of smugglers started the engine and pushed off away from shore. The man at the helm then jumped off the vessel into the waist-deep water, shouting vague instructions about how to operate the outboard motor. The dinghy circled aimlessly, and the frightened refugees cried out. Raahel held Yawsep closer, afraid he'd be hurt in the endless jostling. Finally, Lonan took the helm. Raahel knew he'd never piloted a boat, but after a few moments, he turned the vessel and headed away from shore, toward refuge.

The wind whipped against Raahel's face. It stung her eyes and cut through her wet clothes, chilling her further. She clutched her son close against her chest. Cupping his head with her hand, Raahel shielded Yawsep's face against her body. For the first time since boarding, she was grateful for the crush of others and the bit of warmth they provided. The roaring outboard motor and sound of the hull as it skipped and slapped against the waves drowned any chatter around her. Lonan stood at the back of the boat helming their journey, but she could barely see him through the throng of fellow refugees—Christian and Muslim alike—that separated them.

Raahel touched the tiny jar of strawberry jam she'd hidden beneath her blouse, a treat she'd snuck aboard for Yawsep. She knew that a spoonful would calm him down under any circumstance. Lonan wouldn't approve. His instructions had been specific: pack only essentials. But for Raahel, the preserves were essential. Made a year ago from her mother's recipe while Yawsep quickened in her womb, the jam was more than a sweet treat. It was a promise. It was hope. Canned and labeled before trucks filled with corpses began to roll through the streets, it was the taste she remembered before the grit of the first of the bombs polluted the town's air with a rancid metallic tang. Raahel was happy that Lonan hadn't discovered her precious stash; this one small object brought comfort—a taste of the home she once knew and would never see again.

Dark water splashed over the edge of the dinghy, drenching Raahel, punishing her for being a land creature, a foreigner in its surf. She sighed. It wasn't the sea that made her feel like an outsider. It was life. Despite the cold, her face burned. She wondered if people would ever stop shouting, *go home*. Raahel thought, *if only I could*. She regarded the ache deep in her bones as a sign that she'd never see Syria again.

Raahel sought to catch her husband's eye. She shouldn't have turned away before. In Lonan's gaze, she found solace, but now his back was to her, looking toward Greece, hand tilling the rudder like a man plowing the fields for their future. She squeezed Yawsep and thought, *it's okay—as long as they're with me, I'm home.*

The vessel turned sharply, and one of the passengers fell against Raahel. Yawsep started to cry. The dinghy skipped over the swells, bouncing as its propeller howled.

"Shh," Raahel said, but Yawsep couldn't hear her over the keening engine, couldn't feel his mother's gentle bounces over the harsh waves that tossed the boat.

Metal on glass. Raahel felt the hull connect and strike a solid object. The engine cut out, and they were airborne. The dinghy glided above the water. Its own momentum pushed the craft forward through the air until gravity slammed it back into the sea. A wall of water crested over the side of the boat, casting the occupants aside like a blast wave from a barrel bomb. Raahel lost her hold on Yawsep. He flew from her arms onto the body of one of the fallen passengers.

A moment's silence was followed by cacophony. Yawsep wailed. Everyone on the boat spoke at once.

"Yawsep!" Raahel said. She reached down, caught hold of his vest, and pulled him back onto the relative safety of her lap.

"Another boat," someone shouted. "We're going to die."

"Djinn."

Raahel searched the night, convinced they'd collided with something. She saw only dark swells. No signs of another vessel or evil demons riding the surf.

She kissed Yawsep repeatedly. "My love, my baby boy."

"Start the boat!"

"I'm trying!" Lonan yelled.

The engine clicked and whined but refused to turn over.

The wind howled.

Raahel loosened her vest, wriggled her fingers beneath, and procured the hidden treat, only realizing in the moment she turned the lid that she'd forgotten to pack a spoon. Raahel quickly dipped two fingers into the jam, stashed the jar away, and then pressed her fingers to Yawsep's lips.

"Strawberry," she whispered.

Yawsep's cries abated as he sucked the sweetness. Raahel, lost in the moment and already soaked to the bone, didn't notice she was knee-deep in water until the shrieking began. Raahel's neck and arms turned to gooseflesh as she realized her fellow passengers were not producing the screams. Instead, the sounds arose from the water that enveloped them. The confused passengers huddled closer together, pushing toward the center of the dinghy as it took on more water. A female passenger yanked Raahel's arm, dragging her away from the edge of the boat.

"Look out," she said, eyes wild.

Raahel pulled away from the stranger and fell to her knees. Still clutching Yawsep, she cried out for her husband. "Lonan! Lonan!"

Raahel felt a pinch upon her arm from the same woman. She pointed, and Raahel turned in the direction of the woman's gesture, to where Raahel had only just been seated. Hands that may have once been human rose from the sea and gripped the boat's rubber fender with fingernails resembling the talons of a mythological harpy. More hands appeared and latched on all around the edges of the boat. They were surrounded. The hands were attached to arms, arms to bodies, and bodies to heads. The creatures, for none aboard would dare call them human, looked upon the bewildered passengers with hollow interest. Rather, they seemed intent upon taking refuge aboard the boat, their sharp nails puncturing the rubber fender as they fled their watery graves.

Raahel backed away from the specters, whose faces and garments bore such a resemblance to her fellow passengers that she could only distinguish one from the other by the pallor of their skin. She backed away until she could go no further. The living pressed tightly against one another like interlocking puzzle pieces.

The dead continued to board.

Raahel turned and shoved against the other refugees, forcing a space open where she could squeeze and hide Yawsep.

Then the dead moaned. Voices erupted from mouths frozen in rictuses.

"Save me." The dead woman wore a hijab whose tattered fabric exposed her lank, algae-covered hair.

"Mama!" The deceased boy couldn't have been more than five, but his tiny fingers were as powerful and damaging as all the rest, shredding the boat's outer core as he boarded.

Raahel squeezed Yawsep, afraid that her baby would meet the same end. "Please, God!" another lifeless creature cried. "Spare us."

The boat listed, heeling portside as the living retreated from the dead. The sudden shift in weight proved too much for the flimsy vessel, and it began to sink. Waves as big as houses slammed the boat. Raahel was thrown backward and washed overboard, Yawsep torn from her arms.

"Yawsep!" she shrieked, swallowing seawater. "Yawsep!"

Flailing bodies tumbled into the water around Raahel. She could no longer tell the pleas of the living from those of the dead.

Something nearby caught Raahel's attention. The flotation safety ring, and next to it, Yawsep floating on his back.

"Yawsep!"

Kicking her shoes off, Raahel swam toward her son. Her life jacket hobbled her effort, and she lost sight of Yawsep with each passing swell. Finally, he was at arm's length.

"Mama's here," she called out.

Inches from grasping hold of his vest, a gurgled voice, more water than words, spoke. "My ... baby."

Bone-white fingers wrapped around Yawsep's torso and pulled him beneath the water, tight toward an empty bosom.

"No!" Raahel screamed. "He's not yours!"

Raahel clawed at the hands, peeling away icy flesh that didn't bleed until she wrested Yawsep away and pulled him to the surface. Yawsep choked and coughed up saltwater. The wraith rose high above the sea. It held its arms like a woman cradling a baby and began to rock them back and forth. Then, a wild, guttural, animal sound loud as an exploding bomb poured from the creature's open mouth as though its soul was being disgorged. There was no time to comfort Yawsep. Raahel lunged for the safety ring, tucked Yawsep inside, and pushed the ring ahead of her as she swam away from the thunderous howls overhead. Raahel did not stop until her lungs burned, and she could no longer see or hear the wraith. Moving Yawsep to lay atop the safety-ring, out of the water, she ducked under and slipped into its center. The temporary warmth the burst of exercise had given Raahel eked back into the water. Her teeth chattered, and though she placed her arms around Yawsep, he also shivered.

Raahel checked his fingers, toes, and face, crying as she kissed him over and over, swallowing her sobs. If anything happened to him, she would allow the water to take her too.

Cries for help rang out all around Raahel, but since she couldn't distinguish the dead from the living, Raahel remained silent. She floated, afraid to make the slightest sound that might draw unwanted attention from the wandering spirits. The moon set, the night darkened, and the sea fell silent.

Hundreds of bodies bobbed all around Raahel, far more than a single dinghy could have carried. Raahel whispered a prayer for the dead. When Raahel's grandfather died, her mother hastened to bury him in consecrated ground. "Otherwise, he cannot rest," she'd told Raahel. "He might not even realize he's dead."

Raahel made the sign of the cross. She couldn't let Yawsep die here. Over and over, Raahel whispered the opening verses of Psalm 27. "The Lord is my light and my salvation; I will fear no one. The Lord protects me from all danger; I will never be afraid. When evil people attack me and try to kill me, they stumble and fall. Even if a whole army surrounds me, I will not be afraid; even if enemies attack me, I will still trust God."

Though she knew they still dangled beneath her in the murky water at the ends of her tingling legs, Raahel no longer felt her feet. Numb is good, she thought, it comes after pins and needles, it deadens the pain. She hummed a hymn, cradling Yawsep against her bosom, but had no warmth to offer. Occasionally he opened his eyes or whimpered. Raahel dipped her fingers back into the jam jar. As she filled Yawsep's belly, her hopes and promises converged as she realized the jam's real value: it could save her son.

Movement caught her eye as a body she recognized rose from the water. "Lonan!"

Even as she spoke his name, Raahel knew her husband was gone. She thought she saw a spark of recognition in his eyes before he slid back beneath the brackish water.

"Husband …" the word stuck in her throat.

Moments later, something grabbed her feet. Raahel tried to free herself but then felt the strangest sensation. Warmth. Where before she'd had no feeling, the flush of warmth flooded through her, traveling up her legs, saturating her body with a profound sense of peace. She draped herself over Yawsep, and felt the love flow to him.

"Daddy's with us now," she whispered.

———

Startled awake when Lonan released his hold, Raahel opened her eyes to a gray world. Night was over. Soon the sun would rise. Yawsep was already awake, or maybe he'd never slept. He began to fuss as soon as he realized Raahel was watching him. Lonan, now among the sea's undead populace, emerged a short distance away and watched Raahel scrape the jar's bottom with her fingers.

She fed the last bits, more syrup than fruit, to Yawsep, then looked at Lonan. "My little secret," she said.

Yawsep giggled and wriggled his fingers toward the being that, only hours ago, had been his father.

Raahel closed her eyes and said a prayer for Lonan that he might find peace in this his final resting place. She reopened her eyes just as the sun crested the horizon. Lonan dove beneath the water, fleeing the shimmering sunlight that skittered across the surface like skipping rocks.

Raahel gasped. Her tears were a thimble of grief in an ocean of sorrow, but they were warm, thanks to Lonan.

A horn blared, and Raahel scanned the water. A fishing boat headed their way. She recognized the Greek lettering on its hull.

"We did it, my love," she whispered. Giving Yawsep a quick squeeze, Raahel began to call for help.

THE SEAMSTRESS

Russell Reece

IMAGINE THIS. It is seven o'clock in the evening on October 30, 1975. You are looking into a bungalow in a subdivision near a grimy mill town in western Pennsylvania. The house has a small entrance foyer, two bedrooms, a kitchen, a living-room/dining-room combo, and a bath. There are two entrance doors, one on the side entering into the kitchen and another in front. The house is simply furnished with old, second-hand furniture. It is clean and neat. A calendar hangs in the kitchen with today's date circled in red. There are no knickknacks, no paintings on the walls. A World War II photo of a soldier and a pretty young girl sits atop a bureau in the bedroom where a rented hospital bed has been set up and where a large man lies on his back staring at the ceiling.

—

Mary Bix enters the kitchen. She is a frail, gray-haired woman in her early fifties. Her drab, calf-length housedress hangs loosely on her thin frame. Her hair is tied in a bun, her face is plain, her mouth turned down at the corners. Her eyes are tired and milky from a lifetime working as a seamstress. She looks at the clock on the stove and rubs the palm of her outstretched hand on her hip as she is prone to do when she is nervous. She glances at the small packed suitcase sitting by the front door and then walks into the spare bedroom where her sewing is done and where her pullout bed is tucked against the wall. She picks up a spool of heavy thread, scissors, a needle, and the bag of cosmetics she has just purchased at the local pharmacy. She stops for a moment in front of the window overlooking the drive and recalls the month before when she had seen the police car arrive. Mary knew they had come to arrest her, but she didn't care. Imprisonment would have been preferable to being with John again. But rather than an arrest warrant, the officers had brought news. John had been in an accident.

She would smile about it now if that were her way.

Mary walks into the bedroom where John lies immobilized by a spinal cord injury. His eyes follow Mary as she checks the IV drip and then places the sewing material and the bag on the table next to the bed. John's bottom lip quivers as it has done since he was brought home from the hospital only three days ago. The visiting nurse said the trembling was to be expected.

Mary picks up the photograph of their wedding day. She was 19, John 23. They had met and married when John was home on leave. Whenever she looks at the portrait she tries to remember how it was then. She had been happy, she remembered that. Her love for John had grown while he was away at the war in the Pacific. She was so relieved when he made it safely home. Joy had surrounded those first days after his return, and for many years she was able to recall that, at least in part. Even when the drinking and the abuse had started, she used to be able to take solace in those feelings, pull them in when needed. That was a long time ago. Nothing remained of that life but the photograph.

She glances down and catches John's gaze. He is done with the slapping and manhandling, done with the demeaning insults and the booze. Done with everything.

Mary continues to stare at John, no change in expression, as she recalls Darla—

dark hair, made-up eyes, and scarlet lipstick. Mary remembers all too well the night when John had done the unthinkable and brought the stranger to their home. Had forced Mary into her sewing room, threatening to kill her if she ventured out. Soon Darla's giggle and John's deep voice rose and fell in fits of passion. Drunken taunts followed.

"You're an ugly smudge of a woman," John had said. "You belong in that goddamned room. Sewing is all you're good for."

John and Darla had laughed and stayed in the bedroom for hours. Mary buried her face in her pillow as her fear of John turned to unchecked hatred. She knew that nothing would ever be the same again.

John gazes around the room and then stares up at Mary, a sudden realization in his eyes. "It was you," he whispers, breathlessly.

Mary thinks back to the night in front of Rapa's Tavern, one month earlier, as John walked across the street toward his car. He was alone, perhaps too drunk for Darla. Mary had hoped to run them both down but it was just John, moving slowly in the cool evening. His car was parked beyond the wash of the streetlight and she had timed it perfectly, her car upon him before he could react. She had delighted in his terrified expression, the way his hands had slowly reached toward the front of her speeding car like a frightened child. She wanted John to know it had been her, hoped that in the half-second before her car snuffed out his life he would have seen her and would have known.

Only John hadn't died.

At first Mary felt delighted. It had worked out better than she could have hoped. No one suspected her, and John had no memory of the event. He would be confined to a hospital bed for the rest of his life, nurses rolling him over twice a day to change his diapers, nothing for him to do but stare at the ceiling. John's would be an empty life, just like the one she had lived for the past 30 years—a fitting end for a cruel, heartless man.

It soon became apparent that John would require constant care, the kind provided in a home for invalids. He had no insurance and there was no other money. Mary's job as a seamstress barely left her with enough to survive. The state agencies were little help. Her church offered to fund a visiting nurse a few days a week but the rest would fall to her. She felt as if John were abusing her all over again.

John was transported from the hospital to the home he and Mary shared. Upon reflection, Mary was happy. The hit and run had been impulsive. It would have been too kind, too abrupt a payback for everything John had put her through. *This will be much more satisfying*, she thought. *I won't get away with it this time, but I don't care.*

Mary sits down on the tall stool next to John's bed, leans on his chest, and stares into his eyes.

———

Imagine that you are John looking up at Mary, the timid mouse of a woman you have ruled over for the last 30 years, the skinny hag you were embarrassed to be with, who has always shied away avoiding contact, who has been so meek and subservient it sickened you and drove you to dole out even more abuse. Here she is daring to lean against you, staring down with some weird expression that should be slapped off her ugly face.

"Get off me," you say.

Mary pounds your forehead with a closed fist. You grit your teeth. You want to grab her scrawny neck and throw her to the floor, grind her face with the sole of your shoe … but you can't move. You'll never be able to move. Your lip quivers. You squeeze your eyes closed as she whacks you again. You have no way to avoid her blows. You open your eyes. Your heart races.

She opens the bag of cosmetics and retrieves a lipstick and a small plastic pallet of black eyeshadow. "This is what you like, isn't it?" she says. She gouges out a clump of eyeshadow with her fingertips. It crumbles onto your white undershirt as she smears it in one stroke, like a child finger painting, over her closed lids and into the arches of her brow. She wipes her fingers on your chest. She removes the lipstick cap and, still staring at you, applies it to her lower lip and upper lips. You've never seen Mary with lipstick, and then you recognize the color. Darla's color. Your heartbeat quickens.

"What are you doing?" you say, but Mary clenches her jaw and whacks you again. You glimpse her teeth through the scarlet lipstick which looks bloody against her pasty skin. She smears it beyond the lip line past the corners of her mouth into a jagged ghoul's mask from a house of horrors.

A frightened, sinking feeling runs through you as you gasp for air. "Crazy bitch," you say, lips trembling.

Mary raises her shadowy brow and nods agreement. "Are you worried?" she asks.

You *are* worried but you don't answer. You won't give this hag the satisfaction. "You should be," she says.

Mary swipes the bag and makeup containers with the back of her hand. They clatter against the wall and onto the floor. Her eyes flare and her teeth show again as she glares down at you.

Your pulse sounds in the back of your head as you watch Mary unwind a length of thick thread from a spool, cut it expertly with a pair of small scissors, and thread it onto a needle. You see her practiced finger and thumb pull a knot into the end of the thread.

"What ... are you doing?" you whisper.

With the needle poised in her right hand, Mary pinches your trembling lip with her left thumb and index finger. Imagine the wasp sting of the needle, the sound as the coarse thread pulls through the flesh of your lip, and then the tug, and the needle coming down again, the tip of Mary's tongue in the corner of her painted mouth as she pierces your upper lip and pulls the thread taut. And then into the lower lip again and through the upper. She repeats this action seven more times until your mouth is sewn completely closed. She finishes with a double stitch and a hard tug. The force jerks your head from the pillow. She snips the thread.

"I've wanted to do this for years," she says.

Your heart is pounding so hard you think it will break through your skin. Tears stream down the side of your face and your chest heaves as you breathe heavily through your nose. Mary looks down, appears to admire her work. She wipes trickles of blood off your chin with her open hand and then cleans it on your undershirt. Mary's forefinger and thumb grasp your nose. She squeezes. Her eyes are wide again, lips parted in anticipation. Your chest tightens, your eyes bulge and your head begins to pound as you strain for breath. You want to scream, to beg her to stop. You can't speak. You grunt and whine like a whimpering dog. Mary releases her grip and you draw a long raspy breath. She smiles.

You've haven't seen Mary smile in years. This frightens you even more. For a fleeting second you look past the madness and see the pretty girl of 30 years ago, the moment you arrived home from the war, when she met you at the front door and momentarily collapsed in her excitement.

A second later the hag is back and Mary's scarlet lips part in concentration as her thin fingers reach toward your left eye. You moan a scream, blink, squeeze your eyes closed. She roughly pinches your eyelid and stretches it open before releasing it. You blink away tears and whimper for her to stop. She looks at you and nods.

"I understand, John. Really, I understand. But I've more sewing to do before this is over. That's all I'm good for. Isn't that what you said?"

Mary knots the thread in the needle again.

———

Hours later Mary stands by the living room window awaiting a taxi. She'd finished with John 45 minutes ago, after sewing his second nostril closed and watching his head quiver and his face turn blue against the bedsheet. With his final heartbeat, the anguish of 30 years was gone. Mary felt overcome with a rush of peace and calm. She showered and dressed for her trip to San Diego. She'd always wanted to visit San Diego, to see the world-famous zoo and the California beaches. It was something that John had promised they'd do after they were married. A promise unfulfilled. She would go now, enjoy a few days before she was located and brought back to stand trial.

Mary glances across the street at Mrs. Daniel's house where a candle gutters within a carved pumpkin. She realizes that tomorrow is October 31. Kids will be out with their costumes, knocking on doors, consumed with the spirit of witches and goblins, and delighting at things that frighten them in the spooky night. Mary recalls how John never enjoyed Halloween and would actually chase away would-be trick or treaters. Mary checks her watch. Plenty of time before her flight. She is struck with a sudden inspiration.

A while later headlights approach as her taxi arrives. With overcoat and suitcase in hand, Mary walks to the curb and gets into the back seat. As the taxi pulls away she stares back at her front porch where her husband's severed head has been carefully propped upon the top step.

"Happy Halloween, John," Mary whispers under her breath. She fights back a grin and settles in for the ride.

AUTOPSY REPORT

BERNIE BROWN is an Iowa farm girl transplanted to Raleigh, North Carolina. She has published nearly 40 short stories and essays, sews well, and plays the harmonica badly. She holds both a bachelor's and a master's degree in English from the University of Nebraska at Omaha, and is a Writer-In-Residence at the Weymouth Center for the Arts, and a Pushcart Prize nominee. In 2019, her short story, "The Best Shot," set in Iowa, was published as one of the contest winners of the Grateful Steps Publishing contest. Brown's debut novel, *I Never Told You,* was released in October 2019 by Moonshine Cove Publishing. Her Iowa childhood, travels in the States and Europe, and her contemporary life in Raleigh influence Brown's writing.
More at berniebrownwriter.com.

ELLIE COOPER is a native Texan who lives and writes in Austin. Ellie's passion for the written word began in high school, and although she wrote secretly throughout her life—early mornings or late at night between the demands of work and family—it was only after being laid off three years ago and retiring that she dusted off old pages, took creative writing classes, and began writing anew. Influenced at an early age by Southern Gothic writers, Ellie feels that you can find horror in the ordinary where innocuous events, a wrong decision, or heightened emotion can become the material of nightmares. Ellie's work centers around those flawed, dysfunctional relationships between men and women that often become dangerous. Besides writing, Ellie enjoys spending time with her husband, gardening with native plants, hiking the greenbelts around Austin, and visiting state and national parks in an RV camper. Ellie's writing has appeared in numerous publications including *Rio Review, Mused Literary, 2 Elizabeths*, and *Untitled Voices*. Ellie is currently pondering/writing a longer piece of fiction..

DAVID W. DUTTON is a semi-retired residential designer who was born and raised in Milton, Delaware. He has written two novels, several short stories, and 11 plays. His musical comedy, *oh! Maggie*, created in collaboration with Martin Dusbiber, was produced by the Possum Point Players and the Lake Forest Drama Club. He wrote two musical reviews for the Possum Point Players: *An Evening With Cole Porter* (in collaboration with Marcia Faulkner) and *With a Song in My Heart*. He also wrote the one-act play, *Why the Chicken Crossed the Road*, commissioned and produced by the Delmarva Chicken Festival. In 1997, Dutton was awarded a fellowship as an established writer by the Delaware Arts Council. In 1998, he received a first-place award for his creative nonfiction by the Delaware Literary Connection. His piece, "Who is Nahnu Dugeye?" was subsequently published in the literary anthology, *Terrains*. More recently, Dutton's work has appeared in anthologies such as *Suspicious Activity, Solstice, Halloween Party 2019, Equinox*, and *Aurora*. In fall 2018, Dutton's third novel, *One of the Madding Crowd*, was published by Devil's Party Press. In 2019, it was awarded best original novel by the Delaware Press Association. Dutton, his wife, Marilyn, and their Rottweiler, Molly, currently reside in Milton. More at dwdutton.com.

JAMES GOODRIDGE was born and raised in the Bronx. Now living in the Yorkville section of Manhattan, Goodridge has been writing speculative fiction since 2004. After

10 years as an artist representative and paralegal, he decided in 2013 to make a better commitment to writing. Goodridge is currently at work on *The Passage of Time Saga*, a series of short stories in the occult detective genre featuring Madison Cavendish and Seneca Sue, living vampire and werewolf occult detectives. He has written a series of *Twilight Zone*-style short stories entitled *The Artwork (I to V)*, and runs the Facebook writers' page: Who gives you the Write. Goodridge also pens an annual series of blogs for Black Horror History Month at horroraddicts.net He is a member of the Black Science Fiction Society.

ANDREA GOYAN is a writer, actress, and master Pilates instructor. Her short story, "My Neighbor's a Fucking Monster," appears in the Devil's Party Press anthology, *What Sort of Fuckery Is This?* Other recent work by Goyan can be found in *On Loss: An Anthology, Dirty Girls Magazine* (May 2019), and *Newfound Journal* (October 2018). Goyan was shortlisted for the 2019 Anton Chekhov Award for Very Short Fiction. An accomplished playwright, she lives in Los Angeles with her husband, a dog, and two cats.
More at andreagoyan.com.

ROBIN HILL-PAGE GLANDEN worked for 20 years as a professional actor, musician, and writer/editor in Philadelphia, New York City, and Los Angeles. Glanden edited books for Los Angeles public relations guru, Michael Levine, and several of her nonfiction articles were featured in two Los Angeles magazines. Family matters brought Glanden back to her home state of Delaware, and she's now working as a freelance writer, editor, and performance artist. Her short stories have been published in several *Rehoboth Beach Reads* anthologies, and she has won awards for her fiction from the Delaware Press Association. Her poem, "Change Your Feng Shui, Change Your Life," was published in 2019 in the *Dreamstreets* literary magazine. "Worry and Wisdom" was published recently in the anthology *Delaware Bards Poetry Review*. Glanden is a regular contributor to two of the *Guideposts* magazines, *Mysterious Ways and Angels on Earth*, where she writes true accounts of curious "coincidences" that have occurred in her life. Glanden conducts workshops for writers, and performs her poetry and original music with her husband, Kenny. Glanden also produces cabaret shows and performs in various local venues.

JEFFREY D. KEETEN was born on a farm among the flatlands and the endless horizons of North Central Kansas. He's chased and been chased by tornadoes. He's survived dust storms, droughts, and blizzards. He's been stomped by bulls, kicked by horses, and nearly struck by lightning. He left the farm to earn a degree in English Literature from the University of Arizona. While in Tucson, he worked in a bookstore to pay his tuition, which morphed into a 10-year odyssey of managing stores in Arizona and California. He became part owner of a regional, weekly, farm publication in Dodge City, and every Friday as the paper rolled off the presses, he frequently got high on the smell of hot soy ink and the vanilla scent of crisp, new paper. He also owned real estate and rentals, but has downshifted away from those endeavors to focus on what he deems most important. Keeten is, first and foremost, a reader. A writer of book reviews. A collector of books. He dabbles with writing fiction. Jeffrey's favorite book is whatever book he's currently reading. He watches the sky with his wife and their Scottish Terrier.

More at jeffreykeeten.com **and** goodreads.com/user/show/3427339

HEIDI LOBECKER writes short fiction about weird and wonderful characters in uncommon and unusual situations. She majored in English and takes some of her inspiration from her love of Shakespeare. Living in rural New Jersey, she spends her free time outdoors, hiking, biking, camping, and sailing with her husband and two sons. She works as an IT product manager. Her go-to question is, "Did you test it?"

BAYNE NORTHERN transitioned from writing nonfiction to fiction after publishing an executive summary to "The Future of Independent Life Insurance Distribution," Her prose has appeared in several anthologies including *Equinox, Solstice,* and *Suspicious Activity*. She is currently completing her first novel, *The Bitch Seat,* situated in the financial services industry. An avid short story author, Northern is also an active volunteer with the Rehoboth Village Improvement Association and a resident of Rehoboth Beach, Delaware.

JOSEPHINE QUEEN grew up in England and moved to the US in her early 20s. She now resides in the Northeast with her husband and daughter, writing flash fiction and short stories that err on the creepier side of things. She is making final edits to a middle-grade fantasy novel—which she hopes to have published during her lifetime—as well as a collection of ghost/horror tales. Josephine's writing has been published in *Siren's Call*, *72 Hours of Insanity*, and *Mother Ghost's Grimm* (volume 2) and on websites including 101 Words, Nutshell Narratives, and Christopher Fielden's 81-Word Challenges.
More at josephinewrites.home.blog.

J.C. RAYE'S stories have appeared in anthologies by Scary Dairy Press, Books & Boos, Franklin/Kerr, C. M. Muller, HellBound Books, and Death's Head Press. Other publications are on the way with Belanger Books, Rooster Republic, and Jolly Horror. For 18 years, she's been a professor at a small community college, teaching the most feared course on the planet: public speaking. Witnessing grown people weep, beg, scream, freak out, and collapse is just another delightful day on the job for Raye, and seats in her classes sell quicker than tickets to a Rolling Stones concert. She also loves goats of any kind, even the ones that faint.

RUSSELL REECE'S poems, stories and essays have appeared in a variety of journals and anthologies including *Blueline, The 3288 Review, Memoir Journal, Crimespree Magazine, Edify Fiction, Under the Gum Tree, The Broadkill Review* and others. Reece has received fellowships in literature from The Delaware Division of the Arts and the Virginia Center for the Creative Arts. His stories and poetry have received Pushcart and Best of the Net nominations, and awards from the Delaware Press Association and the Faulkner-Wisdom competition. He won the Pat Herold Nielsen Poetry Prize in Chester River Art's 2019 Art of Stewardship contest. Russ lives in rural Sussex County near Bethel, Delaware on the beautiful Broad Creek. More at russellreece.com

LINDA RUMNEY started writing after a painful break-up, a near-miss nervous breakdown, and a discovery that she'd spent a lot of time making others happy while being miserable herself. Since 2011, Rumney has written nine feature film scripts, seven short film scripts (two of which she directed and produced and were subsequently inducted into the National Screen Institute of Canada), two novels (one that took her to the Squaw Valley Writer's Community in 2018), and a collection of short stories. Rumney currently works as a palliative nurse clinician, guiding and supporting patients and their families toward a "good death."

ELIZABETH VEGVARY studied creative writing at California State University, Sacramento, before dropping out to manage the import section of a famous record store and misspend her youth. Years passed and now she lives in a small enclave in the foothills of the Cascade Mountains. When she's not taking long walks in the dark woods with her husband and her dogs, she's far too often wandering alone with her thoughts. She's been writing for most of her life, absent a two-decade sojourn to raise her babies, become a certified lactation educator, and hang a professional photographer shingle. Currently life is smaller, but the words are bigger. Elizabeth manages her husband's business and edits a monthly parenting magazine. Her work has been published by Zoetic Press, Rozlyn Press, and has appeared in *Oberon Poetry Magazine.*

Made in the USA
Middletown, DE
12 October 2020